Mane Chance

A Soulstealer Novella

NICOLETTE REED

EPub Edition July 2014 ISBN: 978-0-9905617-0-5
Print Edition ISBN: 978-0-9856401-9-4

PRAISE FOR FAE HUNTER

"Once you start reading Fae Hunter, you won't be able to put it down. The action starts on the first page and never lets up for the entire book. Just when you think you can take a deep breath and maybe even put the book down for the evening, a new twist erupts that makes you keep reading for one more chapter and one more chapter and one more chapter…"

-Romance and Mystery Author and Editor Sally Berneathy

"This book has so many surprises, twists, and turns, I couldn't put it down."

-Paranormal Romance Guild Reviews

"I think it's this love triangle that made the book for me."

-Fantasy and Romance Author J.F. Jenkins

"Great world-building, engaging characters that quickly draw you into the story, and enough twists and turns to keep you flipping the pages."

-Fantasy and Romance Author Crista McHugh

"…if you want a kick-ass heroine who struggles to do her best and save her world then you should definitely check this book – and series – out."

-The Flutterby Room Reviews

TITLES BY NICOLETTE REED

Fae Hunter (The Soulstealer Trilogy, Book #1)
Mane Attraction (A Soulstealer Novella, Book #1.5)
Fae Guardian (The Soulstealer Trilogy, Book #2)
Mane Chance (A Soulstealer Novella, Book #2.5)
Fae Warrior (The Soulstealer Trilogy, Book #3)

One life is all we have and we live it as we believe in living it. But to sacrifice what you are and to live without belief, that is a fate more terrible than dying.
- Joan of Arc

CHAPTER ONE

"Where are we going with this?" Kit trailed her fingers from Mane's bare shoulder down to his waistline. She curled her naked body up against his. A serious question about their relationship veiled by the softest of touches.

He gave a deep sigh and sat up in bed, the sheet falling to the side. Labored steps brought him to the window. Kit didn't understand why he bothered. The view never changed and they were both stuck in Dell'Aria, a garrison in the sky, unable to do anything to fix the problem. Like watching the evening news, a constant barrage of evil parading by and all you can do is sit back and cringe. Mane pushed open the shutters and a cold blast of air caused Kit to bring the sheet up tight around her chin. "I don't know."

The last answer she expected and the one she most feared aside from "nowhere." Since becoming entangled with Mane and the selkie, Kit had tried desperately to hold onto what she used to be.

Human.

Every day the memories slipped further away. She'd gone from juvenile to young woman in one night thanks to

1

the selkie sleep, losing ten human years. Too bad the spell only took her youth and not puberty's emotional roller coaster ride. She regretted losing the first but would have been thrilled to give up the latter.

"Lake Mavrovo is worse." Mane didn't answer her question, concentrating instead on the only thing anyone seemed to care about anymore, what form their demise was going to take. He bent over to get a better look and she watched his sculpted backside. His words concerned her, but needs outweighed reason. They were together only last night, and this morning her hunger felt magnified. Satisfying her sexual needs kept the demon inside her satisfied so it didn't break out and demand blood. Her addiction to Mane made relapsing inevitable.

"Mane, can you come to bed?" After a quick romp she could get her mind back in the game. Every other inhabitant of the Realms was preparing for a battle. Priests, Guardians, even the ice fruit pickers theorized on when the opening bell would sound and which competitors would be stepping into the ring.

Mane stretched his arms to the ceiling and gave a slight yawn, a sparkle in his eyes. The man dazzled. He knew the power of his charm. Better than any boy band crush she ever had as a preteen and built for making love. The soul of a depraved demon animated the hardened body of an elven warrior. All the better. Any excuse for allowing her inner beast to revel in immorality. She and Mane were meant for one another.

"You seem particularly 'hungry' lately. Have I not been satisfying you enough?" Mane starred in all the unrated movies playing in her head. In two steps he dropped to the edge of the bed and ripped the sheet off Kit, letting it fall to the floor. "Come to think of if I'm rather hungry myself this morning."

Mane grabbed Kit's hips and dragged her closer. He dug his fingers deeper into her backside and feasted on her upper thigh.

The demon read her so well. She wanted his affections, but the desires swirling around inside her were more complex now. He deserved the truth.

"Wait." Kit cupped Mane's face and his warm lips momentarily slowed their assault. "Your solution to this little problem of mine isn't working as well as it used to. We need to find another way to take care of things." The satisfying effects of their 'sessions' were becoming short-lived. Something felt wrong. There might come a day when these rituals used to keep her beast under control wouldn't be enough. Then she'd turn into the monster her mother, Queen Elemi of the selkie, always wanted.

"You don't know what you're talking about." He continued his conquest. Words muffled as each slip of his tongue closed in on the gnawing hunger. A new edge to her cravings surfaced right below the limit of Mane's talents to assuage her need. The bloodlust used to be satiated by this type of lust – now sex only riled up the hellion inside her. After the rolling waves of pleasure crashed into her, the worst of her urges would rise from the wreckage.

"If you do this, we'll have to go out and find something to kill. Something bigger than a rabbit." Even as she gave her confession, Kit drew Mane closer, her primal urges taking over. Soon nothing would stop her. She could be standing at the center of a room with a hundred people watching her. It didn't matter. Nothing mattered but him.

That revelation scared her more than anything. Almost. Turning into a blood thirsty monster would always be her number one fear.

Mane withdrew, sitting back on his heels. "You aren't kidding, are you? I thought this would work for longer."

"You're saying my attempt to control my urges is pointless." She retreated to the warmth of the bed and swaddled the sheet around her body, trying to search out a fading sense of security.

"No one can know for certain what's happening to you. You're the first one of your kind. But I've seen the hunger take over before."

The door to their room clicked open. One of the female Guardians stood in the doorway. Steam rose from a tray of freshly baked tungstead root and dried fish in her hands, a delicacy the King generously shared with Mane and Kit.

The Guardian lowered the tray and let out a small squeak at the sight of Mane's full frontal. Mane, of course, did nothing to cover himself and, considering what he'd been up to, he definitely stood at attention.

"I am sorry to disturb you. The King asked me to bring these rations to you at once. He wishes to speak to the both of you as soon as possible."

Mane strode over and took the tray from the fae. She cleared her throat and tried to look anywhere but at his groin, a hopeless task.

The nervous energy rolling off the fae woman acted as an intoxicant. A compelling blend of fear and desire. The beast pounded away at her resolve and a meager meal of meat and roots scarcely satisfied this kind of craving.

"Dismiss the Guardian." Kit dropped the sheet without a care for her exposed breasts and the amulet hanging freely at her neck. If the woman didn't leave immediately, in seconds the taste of blood would be coursing down Kit's throat. The Guardian's eyes widened and she pressed the tray into Mane's hands.

Mane ushered the woman out the door. "You can tell the King we'll visit him shortly. Give us a minute."

The door clicked shut, blocking the Guardian's scent. Kit's arousal closed down.

"We don't have time to hunt. We'll have to do this another way." Mane handed the food to Kit. "Eat this. I'm going to hop in the shower. Both of us should cool down a bit."

A deluge of need threatened to overcome the control Mane tried so hard to teach her. He was right, of course. Her ultimate goal should be to take care of herself. Kit took the knife sitting at the edge of the bed. She grasped the blade and gave a sharp pull, slicing open another wound on her palm. The irresistible impulse to cut appeased the terrible hunger building up inside but only provided temporary relief. Six angry stripes, all made this week, decorated her palm like some sickly candy cane. The healing salve Dooley made for her would run out too soon.

"Good girl." Mane grabbed his satchel and closed himself into the bathroom, leaving her hand bloodied and her heart unsatisfied. Blood or sex helped to keep Kit's bloodlust under control. She much preferred the latter.

☙❧

Walking away from Kit wasn't easy. In fact it was hard. Definitely hard. And damn uncomfortable. Mane sat on the edge of the porcelain tub and shifted his erect cock. The intoxicating scent of her desire played upon his senses, scrambling all possibility of reason. He tried to remember to focus.

Mane hoped the noise of the shower covered the sound of him shuffling through his belongings. A shard of the talking mirror provided the only means to speak to their contact Earthside. He kept it with him at all times. Lake Mavrovo's churning waters would soon boil over. The backlash might affect places outside of the Realms. If Kit found out about the level of his concern for Earth she would start thinking about her father, and they couldn't afford any more distractions. The growing threat loomed ever closer, a chilling shadow of evil without a face or a name.

His hand closed around the stiff edge of something deep inside the contents of his satchel and his mouth went dry. Slowly he lifted out the picture of Catherine. Maybe he should be concerned about his own lack of attention. The photograph found its way to him for a reason. A reminder. He caressed the cheek of his lost love, remembering her face, her eyes, her long brown hair, and the strength of her desire for him. Guilt stabbed him in the gut and he fought the urge to clench his fist around the portrait. He didn't deserve to reminisce. His actions foretold her fate. The advent of Ravanna, the Demon King of Acheron, pressed down upon them and Mane planned to get in his way. Kit's devotion to him put her in the line of fire, the same as Catherine.

He propped the photograph on the edge of the mirror and stared deep into those brown eyes as he leaned back and stroked the length of his erection, remembering the last night with his beloved Catherine. They were hot and heavy in the front seat of the Edsel. The intensity of their lovemaking steamed over the windows. Catherine's head tipped back, her mouth slightly open as Mane explored every last inch of her. Her black satin bra swung from the rearview mirror.

She loved to straddle his hips, dipping down to tease him with her heat, forcing Mane to wait for her to be ready. Catherine's lessons taught him the basis of what he hoped to pass on to Kit. Restraint. In small doses his former lover helped turn him from a monster to a master.

In moments like this he let go a little and allowed his hands to wander. She counted on it. Fresh from a night out at the club, neither one of them could wait to make it to his apartment. The image of Catherine rubbing against his erection formed in his mind, her voluptuous breasts swaying just out of his reach. Mane continued to massage the length of his shaft, his peak imminent.

He remembered Catherine ripping aside the small square of fabric and thrusting him deep inside.

Then it happened. Mane allowed himself to close his eyes. To relish in the moment. To lose control. He came hard into his hand. The memory then shifted from one of pleasure to horror.

The crushing sound of metal as the car door ripped from its hinges. Catherine violently torn from his lap, the icy chill of the midnight air slapping him across the face. A white hot blast of magic immobilizing him. Watching, powerless, as they dragged her away, kicking and screaming. The demons took full advantage of her nudity before shoving her by her hair into a waiting van.

Ravanna appeared in the doorway wearing a different face, but Mane sensed the Demon King of Acheron behind his stolen human mask.

"You defied me, Mane. You defied me and she is going to pay for your deception. She's mine to play with now. Not that you'll want her after I'm through."

The spell rendered Mane speechless. His mouth opened and closed but nothing came out. The door to the van slid open and one of the demons called out to Ravanna. Catherine screamed out once more then went silent. "No," he shouted in his head, his frantic gaze shifting out the window, trying to get a glimpse of Catherine. Ravanna was going to kill her and he had placed the target on her back.

"Hold the bitch still." A slight growl pulsed through each of his words. "You won't be returning to Acheron. Don't bother coming after her. I can't kill you, but I can banish you and take this pathetic form of yours."

Ravanna pressed his finger into the palm of Mane's hand and it cut like a knife through butter. Pain ripped through him as blood coursed down his arm. Ravanna laughed at his agony. "I'm sending you into the body of a newborn elf in the Realms where I can watch you."

Ravanna grabbed Catherine's bra from the mirror and pocketed it. "You aren't allowed any more toys."

He slammed the car door, and suddenly the memory burst into a million pieces. The door to the bathroom opened.

Kit's attention went from Mane's hand to the picture. Without a word she slapped him across the face.

"Wait." Mane choked on his own words. Kit didn't hit him with magic but her blow stunned all the same. She stormed away, a torrent of blue hair sweeping out the door before it abruptly slammed shut. He looked into the mirror at the handprint she left behind. A single hot tear ran down his cheek, across the smear of blood. "I never wanted this to happen."

Words not only for Catherine but now for Kit.

CHAPTER TWO

Kit stormed out of the room, her anger changing to hurt. Jerking off to another woman's picture, what the hell? The magazines she once found under her father's bed were full of nude women in tawdry poses who left nothing to the imagination. Tits and ass she could handle. This photograph had been different.

A fully clothed woman, looking happy and smiling for the camera. Smiling for Mane? Most likely another girlfriend. He had been her first boyfriend, her first everything. How stupid of her to expect their relationship to last.

Kit rounded the corner and nearly ran into Dooley, his chocolate brown eyes more tempting than the sweet confection. Her friend Valora was lucky to have two men fighting over her. Better than wondering whether the one you have is in love with you or not.

"Whoa. Kit, where you off to so quick?" Dooley caught her by the arm as she tried to shoulder around him. He didn't ask to get caught up in the drama between her and Mane, but she couldn't hide the tears in her eyes.

Searching for something to explain them, she showed

him the cut on her hand. "To see you. I ran out of the healing salve you gave me. Can I get a refill?"

"Sure, follow me. I'm on my way to the arena to practice. We can stop at my chambers. I'm sure I can get something together for you."

Kit trailed behind Dooley and traced the lines of muscle in his broad shoulders. The men around here never wore shirts which made keeping her bloodlust under control near impossible. But the idea of sinking her teeth into demon flesh made her sick. Her menu didn't include Dooley or Mane. Even knowing this, the urge to consume him overwhelmed her.

Only one more corner remained until they arrived at his door. Another body might sate her hunger. She had to catch him by surprise, however, because Dooley knew magic. One of his spells might be able to stop her. She counted on her powers of selkie seduction to persuade him. Plus, most men easily give in to a naked woman straddling them. The chase thrilled, but only the capture would satisfy. *Hopefully*.

She feigned tripping over something in the darkened hallway and instinctively shot her injured hand out to brace herself. The gritty wall acted like sandpaper on her fresh wound. A cry of real pain escaped her lips.

"Kit, are you okay?" Dooley rushed to her side and she didn't hesitate.

She used her arm to encircle his neck and pulled him into an embrace, her other hand locating his manhood. Through the stiff fabric of his jeans he grew stiffer. Her severed morale code screamed across the abyss between thought and action. Dooley belonged to Valora. What she was doing was wrong. Her selkie lust turned up the volume, drowning out the voice of reason until only a dull thudding need remained. "I'm much better now."

"Kit, what the hell are you doing?" Dooley grabbed her hand, his strong fingers pulling her away, but the bloodlust magnified her strength.

"Exactly what you think I am," she said, leaning over and licking his neck. Mane's teasing had already brought her close to the peak and she rubbed furiously against Dooley's crotch, working the sensitive nub between them.

"Kit, stop," he said, flipping her onto her back. She retaliated by wrapping her legs around his. He arched away from her and she raised her hips, grinding into his body.

"Come on, Dooley. Stop being such a prude. We're both consenting adults."

"And both in love with someone else," he said. The reminder brought the tears back to her eyes. Mane's betrayal should have made her own easier, but it didn't. Dooley continued to struggle. Kit imagined he wanted her. Desired her like Mane should. Tears blurred her vision, reason fighting against the delectable flesh. Her heart pounded, climax imminent. Without warning, a firm hand ripped her off Dooley. The lust drove her into a maddened hysteria and she lashed out at whoever had the nerve to deny her release. A selkie's fury spared no one.

Kit whipped around and froze, caught in Mane's violent stare.

❦

Mane' s heart pounded and the demon rage rose as he held Kit and watched Dooley struggle to his feet then take a few steps backward to put some distance between them. Smart idea.

He held his hands up in surrender. "I'm sorry. She told me she ran out of the healing salve for her hand and then she lost it."

"Go." Mane's order was as much for Dooley's own good as his own. He didn't instigate this encounter or Mane's barely contained wrath. The woman in his arms caused this. His anger rose. She couldn't control herself. He cared too much about her. This back and forth between them only served to weaken their defenses against the real threat lurking in Mavrovo.

Dooley tucked his t-shirt back into his jeans and turned the corner into his room. He possessed firsthand experience of not being able to walk away from someone, even if she drove you out of your mind. Maybe after this was all over the two of them could have a beer and a few laughs.

"I hate you." Kit's small fists pounded at his chest, barely making him flinch. She had power in this state, but he always had more.

"You can hate me all you want, but you need to get yourself under control, Kit. You were dry-humping Dooley in the hallway. Do you want to have to explain yourself to Valora?" Kit might hate him but maybe she would come back to reality at the thought of disappointing her best friend.

Kit went still in his arms and her hand flew up to her mouth. "You won't tell her, will you? Oh God. I don't want her to know. She's been through enough."

"No, I won't tell her and I'm betting Dooley won't either. But if you pull something like that again and one of the guards catches you, I can't control their gossiping."

"Thanks. Thanks a lot." Kit rolled her eyes and forced herself from Mane's hold, retreating down the hallway with a determined swagger.

"You can't leave, Kit. You're in no condition." She hated him right now. He planned to come clean about Catherine, but not until she got herself under control. Her feelings were a mix of lust, jealousy and murderous rage. Feelings all too familiar. But if he let her run around in this condition, guilt and shame would be chasing her instead of him.

"It's not your job to fix me," Kit yelled at the top of her lungs. "You can leave anytime."

Mane lunged, pinning her body between his and the wall. He dipped his head down and whispered into her ear. "One day I hope that is true. For your sake."

He lifted her skirt and slid one finger inside her, eliciting a gasp.

"I can do this without you." Her hand replaced his. Mane continued to hold Kit tight as she stroked her swollen mound. The motion teased his growing erection.

Kit came in his arms, shuddering in waves, her eyes squeezed tight. When she opened them she stared directly at Mane and her lip quivered. "It's not enough. Oh God, it's not enough."

Mane caught her by the elbow and twisted her around, gripping her hair at the nape and tugging backward. "Then we'll try again." He tugged his shorts open and shoved into her, working slowly back and forth. Lovemaking these days came in quick bursts since they were always in battle trainings and debriefings. In fact, the King had sent for them before she ran away from him. Every thrust ticked off another second counting down on the clock. The King had never before sent for just the two of them. Kit's growing bloodlust concerned him. The King's requesting private counsel concerned him more.

From what he could see from his window, the waters of Lake Mavrovo were growing. Red waves overtook the trees that acted as a natural barrier between the selkie and the Riparian Forest, rewriting the laws of magic. Soon all hell would break loose. Literally.

Mane slid his hand over Kit's exposed flesh and pinched her inflamed nub between his fingers, sensitive from her self-induced pleasure. Already ripe from her self-induced pleasure, she moaned underneath him signaling her need for another release, and he gave it to her.

Kit's cries echoed along the stone passageways followed by the crash of metal against rock. From around the corner their morning visitor, the same fae guardian, stood in shock.

She scooped up the tray she had dropped, shielding her face as she spoke. "The King sent me to find you. The matter is urgent. He asked me to personally escort you."

Mane offered a hand to Kit. "Are you going to be okay now?"

"Yes, but I still hate you." She stood up and straightened her skirt, tossing her bright blue locks over her shoulder with a petulant flourish.

"Lead the way. We're as ready as we'll ever be."

CHAPTER THREE

As they got closer to the King's quarters, the murals adorning the halls became more elaborate. Glorious winged warriors sacrificing their own safety for the fae. Each work of art commissioned in homage to a great battle fought and won. To protect the people of Dell'Aria, Kit needed to get off this rock. A temporary return of her control wouldn't assure anyone's safety. Meeting with her mother, Queen Elemi, face to face might be dangerous, but it was a risk she'd have to take. If she ignored her mother's involvement in this, the results could be devastating. Besides, the fact remained her selkie nature made her violent. Her mother had knowledge Mane didn't. Perhaps she could tell Kit how to get control of herself.

"We'll talk soon. I want to explain the picture to you." Mane caught her by the shoulder. She shook him off and continued walking.

"There is nothing to explain. I've seen plenty of those kinds of photos under my dad's bed. I don't do it for you anymore. I'm too much of a burden. I get it. I'll fix it." The King wanted to see her and Mane. Her mother would be a likely topic of discussion. The Queen had to know who turned on the faucet of cinnabar in her lake. If she were alone she wouldn't be worrying about Mane all the time. She already knew how to find prey. The rules Mane made up were just that. His rules. About time she lived by her own. This picture situation provided a convenient excuse to get rid of him.

"What game are you playing, Kit?" This time when Mane caught up to her she stopped.

"Look, whoever it is, I don't care. My problem is bigger than the both of us. And it's not a game to me."

Mane brushed his hand lightly across her cheek. "You seem to forget I offered to help you."

A guard popped his head out from around the corner. "Sorry to interrupt, but the King is expecting you two."

Kit took Mane's hand from her face and placed it down by his side. "I won't let your sense of duty get in my way."

"Are you going to tell me what you mean or do I have to find out the hard way?" Mane jogged after her, but his answer would have to wait until after the King's pronouncement.

The guards in front of the King's chambers swung the door open wide and stepped back to let Kit and Mane pass before them. As soon as they crossed the threshold the door slammed shut behind them.

Even the slumped shoulders of the man at his desk could not hide the glorious wings at his back. Such a contrast to his daughter Valora, born with stunted black wings and unable to fly. And even though Valora liked to pretend they were different, Kit knew the King and Valora were the same. They would both risk themselves to save their people. Some soldiers craved valor and others were motivated by a deep love of their people, their country. Those kinds of soldiers run into the fray even when they know they won't return.

Kit regretted having to leave Valora alone, but she had to. Valora would fight to the death for her friends and Kit had already been responsible for enough destruction.

The King raised his red rimmed eyes from the papers on his desk.

"Your Grace, when is the last time you slept?" Kit took a few steps forward to look closer into the King's eyes and he looked away.

"I'm grateful for your concern, Kit. Please put on your glasses." The King averted his gaze. "It's important you receive everything I am about to tell you without influence."

Kit tried not to let the King's comment get to her. Her selkie powers gave her the ability to mesmerize her victims, but she thought she had earned trust amongst these people. Truth be told, she fit into the same category as Mane and Dooley – demons. She understood his caution considering the imminent threat. Common sense, however, didn't make his rationale any easier to stomach. She tipped the glasses onto her face.

"I apologize, Kit. Things have happened." He shook his head and clutched his forehead, pressing his eyes shut. "Things I wish I could unsee. But I can't. It's my fault."

Mane gestured toward the window that offered a view of Dell'Aria and the tainted Underworld. "Is it Mavrovo? Because none of what's happening there is your fault. I can guarantee it."

"No, it's – I wanted a better idea of who is responsible for this. There is no way to prepare for this battle unless we figure out who we are about to attack. Yesterday I sent a contingent of the guard and one of the priests who has been undergoing magics training. I thought if they got close enough to Mavrovo then we could learn what we were dealing with."

Mane's focus centered on the King's words, his brow furrowed. Even from his tower window the King couldn't hide from the red-washed tree tops of the Riparian. The rate of decay had become much more rapid than the priest's predictions foretold.

She took a step toward the view she'd silently admonished Mane for taking in earlier, placing herself to the left of the King. A heavy tapestry, each brocade panel embroidered with an image of a former Queen of the fae of Dell'Aria, hung on the wall. The faintest etching of Valora's profile, the next in line to take the throne, decorated the center panel. *Valora, the one supposed to save us all, not a pathetic half-selkie with no control.*

"What happened to the soldiers you sent?" asked Mane.

A loud growl came from behind Kit as the tapestry shook and fell to the floor. Hands shot out at her from bars affixed in the wall. A makeshift cell right inside the King's quarters, the prisoner inside even more a monster than she.

࿓

Mane reacted at the same instant he saw the danger to Kit. He bounded over the desktop and pulled Kit out of harm's way. A rotting stench quickly filled the small space. Death.

"That's what happened." The King pulled open a drawer and empty glass vials clinked against one another . He drew out a small syringe full of a dark blue substance and walked toward the outstretched hand. Hunger, not pain, laced the moaning coming from the thing inside. A hunger all too familiar to Mane.

He took a step forward and Kit clutched onto his shoulder. "Don't get too close."

"It's okay." Mane patted her hand. "Let me do it, Your Grace."

The King nodded and didn't fight Mane's request to help. Whoever started this battle won a huge blow today. They were working from the inside out. The King embodied the heart and soul of his people. And King Delos appeared spent and out of options.

Mane faced the fae inside the cell. Ravanna's influence showed clear. Bright red eyes stared back at him as he grasped the fae's forearm and plunged the needle into the muscle. He depressed the plunger and the fae sank to the floor.

"We kept the one. The others I had executed. I'm not even sure how they made it back here in their condition. Maybe there was something left of them in there? I ordered them to save one of them. To find a cure. But Pryn has been unsuccessful so far."

"Your Grace, why did you call us here to your chambers?" Kit stood tall beside him. The young girl he tried to protect was disappearing behind a now sturdy jawline and strong stance.

He knew why the King called them there. He prepared his argument for Kit to stay. Kit crossed her arms in front of her chest, lines of sinewy muscle taut with anticipation. She didn't know her strength and would be no match for Ravanna. Perhaps her mother, but not Ravanna.

"You must travel into the Underworld and find out why this is happening. I would send Dooley along, but my daughter would never allow it. I haven't told her I intend to assign you."

Kit stepped forward. "I will go. The problem stems from Lake Mavrovo. I'm the only selkie available and my mother is there. I am the best one to go on this mission. But

Mane stays here."

Kit could be angry at him, but he wouldn't stand for this risky temper tantrum. "You will not go alone. That's not happening."

"Not happening?" Kit stepped up and pressed her finger into Mane's chest. "You don't get to tell me what to do. I am not your property. Besides, if you go down there you risk your demon taking over when you touch those waters. And I don't have time to save your ass."

Mane laughed and cringed at the same time. She knew the right cards to play. King Delos' fear of Mane's demon becoming a part of this might cause a royal command allowing her ridiculous suggestion to become reality. "Do you have any idea how many years I have lived, little one? I have more self-control in my little finger than most ever gain in their entire life."

"Looked like more than your little finger getting a work out this morning." Kit crossed her arms back over her chest and looked to the King. "What is your decision, your Grace? If he goes I don't go and I'm the one you need."

The King stood up tall and spread his wings wide. "If you think after what I have been through you can hold me hostage, then you are gravely mistaken. It will take both of you to figure this out. I would never allow either one of you to go out alone. Between the two of you, you possess the skills necessary for this mission. Kit, your knowledge of the selkie can't be replicated and, Mane, I believe you understand what we're dealing with." He nodded toward the zombified fae passed out in his cell. "You both must go. If you don't go willingly then you will both be taken into Underworld on my order. Then you will have to figure it out together whether you like it or not."

The King formed his hands into a steeple under his chin,

decision made. No more of his own would be sacrificed. Only one obstacle remained between his order and the mission — his daughter. "How will Valora take it when she finds out you're sending us both to our deaths?"

His retort came quick as a whip. "Dooley is my only other option."

Mane stared hard into the King's steely eyes and saw no bluffing evident. This man had reached the end of his rope. The fact he kept one of these zombified fae captive in his own chambers as a constant reminder of his failure meant there would be no more reasoning with him. If he hadn't been driven mad already, he soon would be.

"No, you can't send him," said Kit. "I won't let you do that to Valora. I'll let Mane tag along."

The King sat down and started to tidy up his desk. "Very well, the two of you will leave immediately. The last of the airships is yours to use. I suggest you start in the Riparian. Check on the dwarves and see if you can find some allies amongst your people, Mane. We are going to require…help, I'm afraid."

"I'll get my things." Kit ignored him as she headed out the door.

The King stood, waiting to speak until she exited. "Make sure Kit comes back alive. I don't know what has happened between the two of you, but she is more important. If you must sacrifice yourself…"

Mane held up his hand. "That's one thing you don't need to order me to do."

CHAPTER FOUR

It didn't take long for Kit to prepare herself. Her clothes below the waist were always on thanks to her selkie heritage and the way she could manipulate the scales covering her body. Short skirt or iridescent leggings, she could be as fickle as any teenager. At least she assumed teenagers were fickle. She had skipped those years entirely.

Kit looked at the half open door to the bathroom. She wanted to see, but she didn't want to see either. Maybe his fading love dampened the power their love making sessions had to control her urges. Made sense. As much as anything else did. She shoved a blade in her bag and slung it over her shoulder.

Mane caught up quickly. He leaned against the doorframe and stared at her.

"What we are about to do is going to be dangerous," he said. "Trust me, please."

"Should have thought about that before you had your little morning delight. Look, I'm going to head to the ship. I'll see you there."

"Yes, you will. I've made sure it won't leave without

me."

Kit shrugged him off and made her way out of the castle. Running through the barren streets of Dell'Aria in the early morning light oddly gave her comfort. She prayed no temptation would distract her. She didn't trust herself around others no matter what she said to Mane. This self-issued challenge tested every ounce of her restraint.

The weight of the knife in her satchel thudded against her back in a steady rhythm as she took the last turn toward the docks.

Movement in the shadows brought her to a skidding halt. Pinpricks of sweat broke out on her upper lip. She shouldn't fear anything in Dell'Aria. Not yet anyway. High above Underworld in the cloud city they were protected, but the feeling of unease remained.

A nearby cart, abandoned of its wares, provided the perfect hiding spot to crouch down and get a better view of whoever or whatever evoked her latent animal response.

A glint of gold and green in the darkness. An argument she couldn't make out the words to. The woman's anger could not be mistaken. Her violent tone echoed sharply against the smooth white marble of the temple. The other figure's voice barely rose above a whisper, lower in tone. A man perhaps?

Before Kit could decide whether or not she should show herself the voices disappeared. Again alone on the street, she walked toward the shadows. Wherever the two had been they were gone now. Only a wall. Perhaps they had never been there at all. Perhaps this was proof of her slippery grasp on her own sanity.

"I thought for sure you would have locked yourself into one of the cabins before I caught you." Kit looked up and saw Mane strutting toward her, so full of himself. Her anger flared and yet as he got closer she knew it would only take a small touch and she would fall back into his arms again. Weak. She was weak. But this mission would teach her the kind of strength Mane could not. Most definitely.

As they got onto the ship, Kit looked around. "What did you do to make sure this ship didn't leave without you?"

"Simple, I'm the only one who knows how to fly this thing and we're going alone."

"You mean the King isn't even sending anyone down to escort us to the Riparian?"

Mane shook his head. "He's lost too many. We're expendable. Let's do our best not to let him think too badly of the dark side."

Mane took the helm and turned the great black wheel causing the sails to draw wide, the wind catching the delicate fabric and lifting it away from the docks.

"It's so beautiful. Sometimes I envy the fae their wings. Their ability to fly anywhere they like. Such freedom."

"Such freedom and they squander it," said Mane.

"What do you mean?"

Mane directed the bow of the ship toward the Riparian, its leaves definitely casting a reddish hue. "The fae can go anywhere. Do anything. Yet they hide themselves in their cloud cities and refuse to help until they are forced. Their cowardice is precisely the reason we are the only ones who can go on this mission."

"But Valora has done a lot to help. She brought the dwarves and the fae together after hundreds of years of fighting."

"And, you'll remember, Valora is not like any of the other fae. In fact, it has been hundreds of years since any fae born like her with stunted wings were allowed to live."

"An evil rule. She'll make sure it never happens again

when she is Queen."

"It's our job to make sure she makes it to her throne."

A long journey to the Riparian stretched out before them. Silence made the creaking deck of the ship seem even smaller. She fought the urge to ask Mane about the woman in the picture. If he didn't willingly tell her, she wouldn't ask.

"A calendar girl usually wears less clothing." The words sneaked out of her mouth in spite of her good resolutions.

So much for not showing she cared.

❧❧

Mane wanted nothing more right now than to tell Kit everything, to have the kind of relationship that made that possible. He adjusted the wheel a quarter turn to the right and corrected the sails to lower their altitude.

He looked down into her mythic blue eyes which perfectly matched the cascade of hair falling in waves down her shoulders. Catherine and Kit held an uncanny resemblance to one another, the only difference being Catherine's hair and eyes were both ashen brown, like volcanic rock hiding the fire burning right below the surface. The color was different, but the fire was the same in his selkie princess.

"It's not like that," he said. "I'll tell you everything, just not now."

She crossed her arms over her chest and turned away from him. Turned away, but didn't leave.

Even though he wanted to tell Kit everything he knew her anger would give her a little edge in this fight. If he told her his whole sob story then she might lose her focus and do something stupid. Besides, part of teaching her control included setting aside emotional indulgence. For the moment.

He tried again. "This is not the best time to explain. The time will come when I can. I promise."

Kit dropped her shoulder and let her backpack hit the deck with a thud. She pressed her fists into her hips and faced him. "Why? We have at least a few hours until the ship reaches the edge of the Riparian nearest Mount Elbrus."

He wrapped one of the ropes controlling the length of the sail around the handle of the wheel. Self-made auto pilot.

"Yes, we have a few hours and I don't intend to squander them on old stories." He took a few steps toward Kit and she didn't budge.

"If you think we're going to fool around then you're sadly mistaken."

"No, no." He sank his fingers into the loose curls at the back of Kit's neck. She let out a deep sigh and her lids grew heavy. If she could read his mind right now she wouldn't be lost in lust, she would be running away as fast as she could. The fact she couldn't meant he had a lot of work to do. And only a few hours to get started.

He grabbed the hair in his hands and jerked, pulling Kit's head back and causing her to lose her footing momentarily.

"What the hell are you doing?" Kit fought against his grip and he caught her by the wrist.

"We are going to practice you taking my orders. If we are going to be down there, fighting side by side, I need to know you won't do anything to endanger yourself or others. If not, I will find a way to restrain you on this ship. Alone."

Kit opened her mouth and then slowly let it close again. Her body complied, but her jaw was set stubbornly.

One step at a time. "Good. The first thing you are going to learn is restraint. We tried this before, but this will be a whole new level. Are you ready?"

He tried to suppress the stirring in his loins. This was not supposed to be sexual, not this time anyway, but his cock didn't care. The thought of tying Kit up went directly to only one place.

Kit relaxed her arms, but her gaze was still wary and intent. "Then where are we going to begin this lesson?"

Mane looked up and down the deck. The ship had not been washed in months since the fae of Dell'Aria had focused their energies elsewhere.

"Right here on this deck. You will wash every square inch of this deck. And then you will wash me but only once you have earned the privilege of doing so."

"Exactly who hit you on the head with the crow bar this morning? Your ego has swollen so much, you might require medical attention."

Mane jerked back on her hair. "This task starts by you learning to control your emotions, Kit. Remember. It is all about control."

Kit looked down at the deck and back up into his eyes, her expression untamed. "Well, if I am going to get started you better let go of my hair." Her mouth closed again on her next comment. Most likely a sassy one. This mission might not be a complete disaster after all.

❧

Kit glared at Mane but bit back a retort. She could only play into this demon's hands right now. Considering it was difficult to move when you had someone pulling your hair she was going to have to do as Mane said. For now. And it might work to her advantage. Besides, they'd had their arguments, but he'd never been such a total control freak before. It was kind of hot.

Mane pointed to a bucket on the deck filled with sudsy

water and then to the scrub brush next to it. "And you're not to wear any clothing."

She pulled her shirt over her head and tossed it to Mane who caught it in one hand. A shimmer pulsed over her lower half as she let her scales fold into her body, revealing her naked lower half. If he wanted a game of control she could play just as hard. Kit knew how much Mane lusted after her, how perfect her body was. Better than any weapon where he was concerned.

"Wouldn't want to get myself dirty too soon anyway." She strolled toward the bucket and knelt down on all fours. Expending energy trying to escape from Mane now would be pointless. She buried the brush in the warm sudsy water. This mission belonged to her. She felt the resounding truth in her bones and within the magic of the amulet around her neck.

The amulet gave her mother the power to track her whereabouts. She would know the moment Kit got close to Mavrovo. Mane could not be there. The selkie warriors would kill him.

Mane and his ego would never let her go alone. For the moment she would go along with his power trip until she could find a way to dodge him. Kit looked down at the small patch she had managed to scrub clean and up the deck toward Mane. He had gone back to steering the ship, but he kept his eyes on her. He always did.

She thrust the scrub brush into the bucket and the surface of the water rippled. *All water leads to Mavrovo.* Of course. As soon as they landed she would find the first lake and dive in. Mane wouldn't be able to stop her. In the meantime she just had to survive his silly commands and not lose her focus.

Droplets of water and soap sprayed onto her naked

body each time she transferred the brush to the bucket and back to the floor again. Suds gathered, trailing down between her breasts, making a beeline for her stomach. She increased her pace. If the soap went any lower the delicious bubbles might trigger her barely restrained desire.

∂∘⋖

Mane drank in the scene before him. Control centered on not giving in to your emotions, and Kit needed to learn that. Probably not the best idea to have her complete this task in the nude. Being a demon meant having urges close to the surface. Dance the line and you're inviting trouble.

The deck sparkled. A fine patina of dirt covered Kit. He watched as she frantically scrubbed the deck with tight, rapid, circular motions. She dipped again and froze, a small moan escaping her lips.

He placed the rope back on the wheel and walked down the stairs to the deck. Kit bent over, her back to him. She had cleaned all but a small corner of the deck in record time.

"Are you okay?"

Kit's lungs expanded and contracted at a rapid rate. She was either upset or extremely turned on. He hoped for the latter. "I think I'm almost done."

"Then why did you stop?"

Kit dropped the brush into the wooden bucket. A thud sounded as it hit the bottom. She gave a flirtatious grin and raised her eyebrows. She would be the death of him in more than one way. "Out of soap."

Layers of sweat and soap drenched Kit's body. "There's enough on you to finish the job."

"What do you want me to do?" Kit brought her hands under her pert breasts. "Rub these all over the deck? I'll get a splinter."

He measured the sun left in the sky. Not much time before they landed. He would work with what they had.

Kneeling down before her, he raked his left hand down her side, splashing the soap from his hands onto the floor. He pressed his right hand down her other side, doing the same. He took one hand and paused above her chest. Kit arched her back in response and he pulled away.

"You were in such a hurry you forgot one important thing."

"I'm guessing you're going to remind me."

He dropped his pants and stood in front of Kit, unable to hide his excitement.

Kit pushed her hand between her legs and brought out a handful of the soapy suds. Her eyes full of heat, she rubbed it down the length of his shaft.

"Is this going to be enough?"

Mane braced himself against the railing as she continued to work him into a frenzy. His mind screamed *stop* but his body had other plans. And then he remembered. Remembered his Catherine again. The passionate woman Ravanna took from him. He also remembered Ravanna's promise to take away any more of his play things.

A horrific daymare jolted him into the past. He never knew exactly what happened to Catherine. However, a human mind didn't remain intact after suffering a visit to Acheron, let alone their body. Kit would not meet the same fate.

He took a step away from Kit and looked directly into the green sparkling eyes of Kali Mirch.

CHAPTER FIVE

Another rejection. Kit stared at the shining planks under her feet and tried to ignore Mane's refusal. Her attempts at manipulating him hadn't stopped the buildup of tension between her legs. She brought her teeth together and bit down on her lip. The pain from her sharpened incisors brought reality back into focus. If he wanted her to beg he'd be waiting a long time.

Mane pulled up his pants and tossed her the shirt she had so recently discarded. Energy resonated through her body, folding the scales back over her lower half. A sharp gasp from behind her right shoulder told Kit they were not alone.

"Well, well. Looks like we've found where you've been hiding. I'm surprised you didn't take this ship for yourself." Mane folded his arms across his chest.

Kit turned and saw Kali Mirch standing in the doorway to the lower deck, weaponless. She quickly yanked her shirt over her head and dipped down to pull the knife from her bag.

Kali raised her hands. "I didn't come here for a fight."

Mane took a step toward Kali. "But you did come here. And at a very inopportune time, I might add. We're about to go to a place where no fae has come back alive. Are you here to offer yourself as a willing sacrifice to the cause? You'd make a good shield." Drinking the life from this traitor would be justified, like putting down a wounded animal. Kit could feel the bloodlust rising quickly. Adrenaline hummed through her bones. The muscles in her thighs tensed like a cat before it pounces.

As if reading her mind, Kali looked around, examining her exit points. There were none.

"You killed almost everyone I care about." Kit felt the animal inside her rising closer to the surface.

"But there are things you must know," said Kali.

For a moment Kit forgot her prime objective. People bargain when they get desperate, but there certainly were things happening under her nose.

"Then hurry up and tell me. I'm in no mood," said Kit. To Kit's surprise Mane stepped aside and allowed her to face Kali.

"You interrupted our little lesson on self-control. If I were you I'd start talking quickly." Mane crossed his arms over his chest.

Kali Mirch had been Valora's best friend and her betrayer. She spared Valora's life but not her emotions. Her best friend's fucked up trust issues had Valora torn between two men. The problem started here. Right here with Kali Mirch. Revenge tasted sweeter than the sweetest blood.

"Time's up." Kit took a few steps forward, the knife at her side. Kali's wings were a means of escape. She needed to be faster.

"You saw me talking to him. In the street." Kali spoke in fragments as she walked backward, closer to the outer railing of the ship. "Aren't you curious?"

"Talking to who?" Kit took another step forward and the entire deck of the ship lurched to the side. Her knife fell from her hands as she stumbled and slid down the decking. She grabbed a rope tied to one of the riggings and stopped abruptly. Mane ran back to the wheel and struggled to level the listing deck. Wind rattled through the planks. Kit dodged a falling crate and watched it bounce once before tumbling into Underworld. She might be next.

"Please help," pleaded Kali.

Kit saw Kali's knuckles go white, her grip on the railing loosening. A few inches to the left and Kali would be able to grab onto the rope.

"Why don't you fly away?" yelled Kit.

"I can't."

Kali's wings were the most magnificent she had ever seen on a fae. She had to be lying.

Kali let out a scream as one of her hands lost hold. Mane's muscles strained as he pushed the wheel forward. Any moment now the ship would level out, her chance to right a wrong lost.

It was now or never.

Kit wiped her hand across her stomach, scooping up some of the last of the suds left over from Mane's chore, and reached out to Kali. "Give me your hand. I'll help pull you up."

Kali hesitated, but her grip slipped again and she grasped onto Kit. She looked directly into Kali's eyes and let the full force of her gaze stun her into silence. "Because of what you did to Valora, you will fall, you will be afraid, and it will hurt."

Kali lost her hold on Kit's soapy hand and tumbled through the air. Her wings merely flapped in the breeze as she screamed out. Seconds later the deck righted itself and Mane's strong arms caught her up and held on tight.

Kali's body disappeared through the top of the canopy of the Riparian Forest. The place where Kit expected to feel the sharp pain of guilt felt only hollow, a deep and cavernous pit of never ending despair which she feared might swallow her whole.

❧

For a moment Mane's heart, the one most demons didn't have, had stopped, the muscles in his arms quivering. It had taken all his strength to right the ship again. Nothing would ever be right again if the scream he heard had come from Kit. Images of what could be had flashed through his mind. Kit dead. Life without her. Repressed rage pounded in his ears.

Then his focus returned and he saw Kit sprawled out on the deck, the rope still in her hands, Kali nowhere to be seen. He folded Kit into his embrace. Kali might have been the one who fell, but he had also. Fallen deeply in love with this woman in his arms. He would stop at nothing to keep her safe.

Kit looked up into his eyes and a single tear rolled down her cheek. "I killed her. Made sure she couldn't make it back up on the deck. What if she had something important to tell us? I did hear two people fighting about something in the alley."

The woman in his arms felt fragile The beast inside Kit struck a death blow today and not just to Kali. Mane didn't want Kit to give up. Feeling in control would give her power. Like she had something to contribute even if it was his intention to do all the heavy lifting on this mission.

"She tried to save her own life by telling stories. Kali

equals trouble. We both know who is really responsible for what is happening in Underworld and Mavrovo."

"Yes, my own flesh and blood. My mother." Kit swallowed hard and buried her head against his chest. "I don't know if I will be able to do it, Mane. If I have to kill her, I mean."

Kit's words echoed his fears. She wasn't ready to do what needed to be done and he wouldn't put her in harm's way. "You won't have to. I'll be knocking on Ravanna's door before you have to face your mother. I will end this."

The jagged stone cliffs of Mount Elbrus came into view. Before long they would touch down at the edge of the Riparian. Good news because their journey began in the morning light and now swathes of purple darkened the sky. An unnatural gloom settled in around them.

Thundering booms reverberated overhead and a shockwave rocked the deck, radiating across the sky and leaving in its wake a dark red aura, mirroring the waters of Mavrovo. The morose rainbow rippled like a great wave splashing its colors across the clouds and against every surface.

Kit's head jerked up and she looked at the sky. "It's started."

"Yes, and we're going to finish it." He jumped up, wiping the rain from his forehead. "Gather your things. We're landing soon. Prepare as best you can for whatever we are going to face down there."

"I lost hold of my knife, the only weapon I had."

"Go down below and see what else you can find. Kali probably brought weapons. Maybe you can find a clue as to what she thought she needed to tell us."

Kit nodded and went below deck. Mane returned to the helm and made a few adjustments to their course, heading for the most open clearing nearest the southern entrance to Elbrus. Hopefully the shaman still lived. The demon possessing the old dwarven shaman might be convinced to give up Ravanna's plan. What other play did he have? Politics didn't interest Niro much, but if something could be worked in his favor he would be willing to help. A demon knows what another demon wants most.

Mane let the wheel go as the ship descended. Reaching his hand into his satchel he found one of the few things he carried wherever he went. He swore he would never have any use for the item, but there was always a first time for being wrong.

Looking at the helm brought back so many memories of his father, the elven father who had raised him and treated him as his own child even though he found out early on Mane didn't possess a normal soul born of the Realms.

One day his father took him out hunting. Usually the eldest and leader of their tribe did not travel alone. But he woke Mane early and snuck him outside their camp before the matrons lit the morning hearth.

"Today we shall make your first kill." His father had a full quiver of arrows and a longbow made of wood. Weapons of the elves.

"I've killed before, Father." Mane never pretended to be one of their own. The second he could talk he spoke his mind, much to the disgust of his elven brother, Torkel. Not a blood brother, but a brother nonetheless. He never told anyone the particulars of his demon nature, nor had he pretended to be naïve to his condition. He had already lived a dozen of their lifetimes. Besides, elves were smart. Lying served no purpose.

Mane's father put his hand on his shoulder. "You have not killed like this. There are experiences left in this world you have not had yet, young Mane. Don't despair. This world holds many wonders and is always reinventing itself. Much like you can do."

The first weapon Mane held as an elf had been presented to him on this first hunt, though his ongoing survival depended much more on skill than weapons alone.

"In this forest many things will attract your attention. Each quarry is a test. Your challenge is to find your target. The King of the Serpents can easily bring down the tortoise. The fight is not fair. Find yourself an equal match. Misfire and you may end up with a fate you were not prepared for."

"Yes, a hand I've been dealt many times over."

Mane's father pointed to movement in the nearby brush. "Change is coming."

In the briar brush emerged one of the most magnificent creatures Mane had ever laid eyes on. A white stag. "Messenger from Acheron." The words were but a whisper on Mane's lips.

He let his arrow fly and it struck its target, right through the heart. Two beats, the animal knelt to the forest floor, one last beat and the deer lay on the ground.

"It has three horns." The three horned stag's beauty awed him. He had heard of them in legend but never seen one in person.

"The power of three."

Mane and his father knelt before the animal and made quick work of rendering all the valuable parts they could bring back to the tribe. Before they left, Mane's father cut the horns from the stag's head. He promised to make Mane a special helm, a good luck charm of sorts.

Today the helm sat upon his head for only the second time. As the airship touched down he hoped its magic would lead them through the forest. Each grain of sand that fell from the hourglass got closer to burying him.

❧

A knife. Any sharp weapon. There had to be something somewhere. The whip hanging at her side was handy, but hardly the brutal force she needed. Kit dug through the many boxes and trunks scattered about the rooms below deck. As a child living in the small apartment with her father she had dreamed of living in a house so large she could spend days exploring each room. Dreams probably common to any child who often had to stay indoors, too sick to go to school or to interact with the outside world.

What she wouldn't give for a small one bedroom apartment right now. There were too many places to go. She could feel the ship descending as the change in pressure made her ears pop.

One left. The room at the end of the hall where the door remained shut. For some reason she didn't like closed doors. Probably had something to do with her cousin's affinity for always popping out and trying to scare her at family gatherings.

The hum of the engines sent vibrations through the balls of her feet and into the pit of her stomach. The engine room door had to remain closed, nothing to fear.

She gingerly touched the knob and then snatched her hand away. "This is silly." *So is talking out loud to yourself.*

They would land soon, and if she didn't act immediately upon impact, she'd lose her chance to ditch Mane. Kit pushed open the door and looked around. If Kali had been sleeping here she sure had made herself comfortable. Unlike the other chambers this one could only be described as opulent.

The fine mica chips lining the walls made them

shimmer. The only source of light came from a round window at the farthest end of the room, making most of the room dark but nevertheless inviting.

In the middle of the room stood a stately four poster bed made of solid copper piping. The room practically hummed with the magic reverberating from the sacred element of the fae of Dell'Aria. Bedding made of a warm, chocolate brown velvet practically called out for her to take a break, if only for a little while. Drapes of the same material hung from the canopy and cascaded down the sides.

Next to the bed a basin large enough to bathe in gleamed with fae copper. Despite the sacrifices being made in Dell'Aria it looked like no expense had been spared here. A single candle sat next to a small table near the bedside and flickered in the breeze from the open door.

Someone had recently slept on top of the covers. The last evidence of Kali, the one who probably lit the candle.

"Do you like the princess's chambers?

Kit jumped at the sound of Mane's voice behind her. Her heart froze and then pounded at the sight of her demon lover. Great horns erupted from the sides and front of his battle helm. He wore his vest of furs, a blade held loosely at his side.

"Valora isn't much for this kind of luxury." She gestured to the bed, trying to suck in a quick breath and regain her composure.

"You seem to be forgetting something."

She surveyed the contents of the room. Opulent, but not practical. "I can't seem to find any weapon. Do you think the dwarves will lend me a blade?"

Mane padded over and put a finger under her chin. "You seem to be forgetting you're a princess too."

"I have no desire to claim my title." Kit shuddered to

think of the time she spent stuck below the surface of Mavrovo. The amulet allowed her to walk freely, but being selkie meant she would never truly be free. Her fantasy of going back to Earth and seeing her father again returned, striking her with a bitter case of homesickness. With one hand on her stomach she calmed the turbulence inside. Problem number one, handle Elemi - after she got a grip on herself.

Mane removed the helm and set his things down before closing the door behind them. The deck under her feet vibrated and then went still. One solitary feather floated down between them, a renegade from the bedding. Mane pinched the tickler between his fingers. No hope of escape now.

"We've landed. But nighttime has already descended. We can't go out there yet. I've secured the deck. We have a night to ourselves. We should really get some rest."

Her heart sank. He didn't desire her. At the same time, the idea of him passing out gave her the perfect plan. If she could get Mane to fall asleep she could sneak out undetected. All waters lead to Mavrovo. She just needed a body of water large enough for her to take a dip in. No turning back. Once she stepped off the deck of the ship she'd keep going. For the sake of them both.

Mane opened his satchel and brought out some of the clippings of sweet cane from the trees in the ice fruit fields. "Would you like a little snack before bed?"

She perched on the edge of the bed and chewed mindlessly on the sugary treat, the wheels of her mind hatching the plan. Mane sat at the edge of the copper tub. Steam rose up from the depths of the pool as it began to fill, casting a fine mist over everything in the small space.

"I don't think you can fit in there. Seems like they made

it princess size, not big muscular demon size."

Mane stood up and offered Kit his hand as the water rose toward the lip of the tub.

"Relax a while. I want to tell you a story."

She clenched her jaw, biting down on the sugar cane. Too bad bath water didn't lead to Mavrovo.

CHAPTER SIX

Usually the suggestion of Kit making her clothes disappear didn't even leave Mane's lips before they were gone. Instead the sweet cane carefully balanced between her incisors looked ready to snap in half. Teeth of a selkie could easily do so. She disappeared behind the dressing screen next to the tub.

"I'm in no mood to stay up all night. Give me the Cliff's Notes version." Kit flipped her shirt over the top, her naked silhouette visible through the translucent screen, before slipping into the steaming bath. Through the water's edge he could see Kit's legs knitting back together into the selkie tail.

"What exactly are Cliff's Notes?" He pulled a stool up to the side of the tub, far enough away so if Kit didn't like what he had to say he would be out of her direct line of fire.

"Sorry, letting my heritage show. I mean I don't want an epic, a short story will do." She continued to bite down on the sweet cane and finally relaxed back into the water, letting her blue hair spill over the side of the copper basin.

"My life has been anything but epic, but it has been long. You must have known I'd been with other women." He paused long enough to judge her willingness to hear the truth of his past.

Kit pushed her hand through the water and brought it up, letting the droplets rain down into the tub as she watched the surface of the water ripple back toward her. "Yes."

"The picture I have is of her. It's Catherine."

"You wish the two of you were still together. Now I know why you agreed to come down on this mission. You think you can free her from Acheron." Kit tossed the sweet cane to the floor and faced him. Anger distorted her features.

"No. She is gone. Permanently gone. Even if I saw Catherine again it wouldn't matter. They targeted her for reasons I won't go into and some I just don't know. What I do know is that..." He struggled to find the words and remembered the hunting trip with his father. "With Catherine I bagged the wrong quarry."

Kit squinted, looking confused. "Did you just make a sex reference?"

Uncontained laughter burst from his chest. Kit always did this to him. A mixture of sweetness, innocence and ferocity that drew him in like the waves to the shore. Catherine never claimed to be sweet and innocent. Together the two of them had been out of balance. Kit mirrored qualities he wished for, one of the many reasons he loved her.

He stood from the stool and knelt at the edge of the basin. Kit saved him and he possessed the power to save her if she listened. He stroked the side of her cheek, brushing his hand through her wet hair. "No. I meant Catherine is not my intended target, not the person I am meant to be with. Something my father once told me. After all these years I finally know who is."

"Who?" Kit's voice came out barely above a whisper.

"It's you, Kit. No matter how much I want to save you from Catherine's fate, it's too late. I already love you. And I won't let anything happen to you. I'd die for you." The words were out. Words echoing everything in his soul he tried to hide from Ravanna and in turn had hidden from the one he loved.

"That's what I'm afraid of. You dying. I love you too, Mane. You're not allowed to sacrifice yourself for me." Kit wrapped her arms around Mane's neck. He stood up, taking her body into his arms. He set her gently on the cushioned surface of the bed, knowing he could never make a promise not to protect her. However, he didn't intend for either of them to worry about that now.

He reached up and felt around the top of the headboard. The fae didn't trust their little princesses. Their hormones raged during certain moon cycles and they needed a way to restrain them lest they hurt themselves or others. Worse yet, spawn a bastard child. He planned on being the bastard tonight with the help of some fae magic.

❧

Kit let herself become lost in Mane's advances. His confession had cracked open the thin shell erected around her heart. She breathed deep of Mane's scent and heard something inside her click into place. More accurately she heard something clicking around her wrist.

"What?" She examined the thin copper band adorning her arm, the only substance that could bind the fae, negating their magic. One tug made all hope of an escape drain away. Fae magic attached the other end of the band to the bed post. Without magic her strength would have easily snapped the bindings. "Were you expecting me to go somewhere?"

Mane smiled and tapped a finger to his lips. She could almost see the wheels turning in his mind. She did have other problems, starting with being tied to this bed when she should be making a run for Mavrovo.

"No, but who knows what tomorrow will bring? Tonight I intend to bring you to the edge many times. Only once you're begging me will I let you go over." The subtle change in the tone of Mane's voice made all the hairs on the back of her neck stand on end. He had never lost control of his demon in front of her and she didn't relish the idea he might lose control when she had no way to defend herself.

She tugged hopelessly on the copper cuff. Without knowing how the magic in the bindings worked she couldn't give up on trying to pull free of them. "Won't happen. I hope you have the key to these."

"Daylight is the key. You're mine tonight." Broad bands of muscle flexed beneath his vest. Many nights she had spent safe in those arms.

Mane clipped her wrist into the other binding on the headboard. Without magic skills, fighting against the binds would only bring about exhaustion. She had a long journey ahead, might as well let Mane recharge her batteries and think of another plan.

"I see you're comfortable. Unfortunately comfort is not the plan tonight. Can you please do me a favor, darling?" Mane rubbed his hand from her waist bone to the end of her selkie tail brought about by the warm bath water. She pulled in a deep breath and let the iridescent scales fold back into her skin making her legs reappear.

Mane fastened a cuff to each of her ankles. A small but sturdy chain affixed them to the footboard.

"Do a lot of fae princesses try to sneak out in the middle

of the night?" The one small window above the bed started to make sense. Rather than protecting those inside from intruders, the round porthole kept those held captive here from getting out.

"My experience with fae princesses is limited. Valora does know how to play hard to get." Mane opened a drawer and pulled out several dark crimson colored candles.

She refused to react to Mane's taunting. The long hard shafts of the candles piqued her curiosity. They had never played with toys before. A dampness formed between her legs despite her best efforts to ignore her active imagination.

Mane swept a long strand of hair away from her face, slowly dipping his head down before bringing his lips to hers. His kisses began gently, moving from her lips to her neck and reaching the spot behind her ear that made her back involuntarily arch upward.

Mane steadied his hand on her hip. "We're going to go slowly tonight. Very slowly."

Her breaths came out in short gasps. Pent-up arousal rocketed her out of the starting gates. Whether blood lust or just plain need, this torture tested her will. Despite knowing she shouldn't pull on the bindings, fine lines of pain blossomed at her wrists and ankles.

"At least give me something now. Please." He wanted her to beg so she would. Anything. She expected the telltale grin to form on Mane's face, a sign of his fading will. Instead his mouth drew into a stern line.

He stood and lit the candles, placing each one into a round holder set into the headboard. Three candles. After removing his vest he took a blade from his satchel. Every movement was delivered in a ritualistic fashion. Mane set the short sword down and then placed a whetstone flat on the surface of the desk.

"You look very beautiful tied up." Mane unlaced the cord at the top of his pants letting them fall open.

She gasped, her hunger building even deeper at the sight of his erect length begging to be touched. Begging to be kissed. A familiar scent overwhelmed her senses as she breathed deep. The wax from the candles pooled around the flaming wick, their spice filling the room.

"Mane, what are those candles made of?" She knew the answer before his response. His eyes held a familiar red glow. His demon.

She watched Mane work the length of his shaft, one hand going to the bedpost to steady himself. "I'm sure you know." He paused and knelt at the side of the bed. His warm hands traveled down her stomach and sank deep into her slick folds, careful not to disturb the swollen nub aching to be touched.

She struggled against her demon. The constant nightmare of trying to push a door closed against a beast much stronger was a losing battle. Eventually her muscles would grow weak and the hand of evil would put a chokehold on her will. "Mane, get those out of here. I don't think I can control myself."

The scent of the cinnabar permeated everything in the room. She watched the bubbling candle wax pooling at the edge. Soon hot rivers of molten cinnabar would spill down the sides, cascading onto her body positioned just below.

Mane's caresses ceased as he stood over her body helplessly bound to the bed. "This is what you wanted to see, isn't it?" Through lids heavy with lust she watched Mane's hand, slick with her desire, close around his shaft.

"Mane." She heard the desperation in her own voice. Darkness descended on the lightness in her soul. A blackened screen clouded her vision. The beast making her entrance. Mane grasped the bedpost, shaking the delicate tapers. Wax splashed onto both arms. Pain screamed through every limb as the mental wall controlling the demon shattered into a thousand pieces. The metal bedposts quaked, but the binds held tight.

Mane leaned over her body, his pace quickening. Her demon stampeded through her psyche, tossing around the carefully placed setting in her mind. Taming this beast took patience and focus. Time. Mane stiffened, peak imminent. She closed her eyes and felt his desire rain down upon her bare stomach.

Before the sensation settled Mane took a candle from the pillar and hovered the barely contained vessel of wax over her naked flesh.

The skin at her wrist broke under the force of strain against the binds. The scent of blood and cinnabar curled through the air like a suffocating smoke. How long before she lost an arm? Would the demon stop fighting before that happened?

"Please. Oh, dear God, please."

Mane cocked his head to the side. Observing her through reddened eyes, the demon gave a maniacal laugh. Any sane person's blood would've turned cold, but Kit's demon had come out to play. And she could play hard.

"You should know by now, little one, I am no God. Oh, no, I am a demon. And I love it." He tipped the candle over, letting the rest of the wax drip over her naked breasts and splash down onto the bedding.

He blew out the wick in the candle and set it next to the bed, giving her a wink as he did so. "For later."

For a brief moment her human soul and her selkie nature stood side by side each looking through one eye. Each observing and then experiencing wave after wave of emotion. Her humanity reached out to her selkie sister. *We need to get through what is to come together.*

❦

Mane wiped some of his fluids from Kit's stomach. He massaged the lubricant into the surface of the stone, watching as his every movement further excited Kit. Indulgence like this was a luxury. What they were about to face demanded strength, all they could get. Feeding time for both their demons.

He would make sure they were absolute gluttons tonight. Taking the sword he worked it back and forth against the stone, quickly sharpening the blade in preparation for the ritual. Playing with Kit all night tested his creativity, finding more ways of release for them both. After they were bound he would follow her through life and death.

He touched his finger lightly to the blade and heard Kit's sharp, panting breaths. Before his flesh left the beveled edge he knew he'd already drawn blood, his little one's reaction to the ambrosia of life unmistakable.

He marveled at Kit's beauty. A hardened shell of cinnabar wax covered her upper chest and nipples. Through her eyes, one black, one blue, he saw the coalescence of the warring factions within her.

Pleasure before pain and then pleasure again, a good motto to live by. He rubbed his hand over the warm wax, fondling Kit's taut nipples. He pinched the tiny buds, cracking the wax coating, relishing the way her back arched in response to his touch.

Kit cried out, the pain from her delayed release becoming too much to bear. But Mane knew she would have to bear much more in the days to come. He needed to show her she could handle any temptation before her. No matter what happened, her demon would concede to her better judgment.

He teased the edges of the wax, slipping a finger underneath and slowly tugging upward. Her skin pulled along with the wax before releasing. Kit bit down on her own lip and screamed again. His demon watched red rivulets trickle down the side of her chin making him instantly hard. He ran his tongue up Kit's neck, lapping the blood before kissing her gently on the lips.

"Be patient, little one. You will get your release. I promise." He brought up the sword and quickly ran the blade across the palm of his hand. Blood filled the shallow wound.

Kit moaned and her sharpened selkie teeth extended, both eyes turning an inky black. Her humanity was bound as tight as the binds holding her to the bed. Lost to her selkie heritage. Soon her human side would do what humans did best, fight for independence from their oppressors. Cast off the chains.

He brought the sword to her hand, slicing open a small wound on her palm. Kit's back arched violently, tears streaming down her face. He closed his wounded palm over hers, allowing their blood to bind them together. She would know his love like the beating of her own heart. The only demons in her future would be the ones standing before her in Mavrovo.

He grabbed the candle from the nightstand. The waxy rod gently parted her folds, the edge entering her about an inch before he pulled it away.

Kit's eyes were dark as the night surrounding them. "I'm going to pull my arm off if you don't fuck me soon."

"Really?" One thrust pushed the base of the candle into Kit up to the wick. She cried out in pleasure as he pumped back and forth, her juices running over the cinnabar wand in his hand. A flick of the wrist sent the candle sailing across the floor leaving room for his aching member to press deep inside Kit.

She screamed out, body going slack before sinking down into the plush bedding. Release no longer necessary, he wrapped a length of cloth around his hand before tending to Kit. The whites of her eyes were visible again, no trace of black left. Her demon had retreated.

"My head feels clear. I thought I would never come back."

He loosened the binds, allowing Kit's arms and legs to rest, and slid in next to her. "I knew you would. I always knew you would. There is something inside you, Kit, something stronger than anything I have ever known."

Kit pushed out her lower lip. "I don't want help from my selkie side. If anything I wish I could get rid of this curse."

"No." Mane put a finger gently under Kit's chin, redirecting her attention. "Your selkie side is not the power behind your strength."

"My human side can't possibly be responsible. Catherine was human and she…" Kit's voice drifted off. The blood bond gave Kit access to his memories. Not exactly like a movie, their connection through the bond gave each other access to deep emotions, past and present. She knew now exactly why he gave up on Catherine, not once trying to save her after Ravanna took her into Acheron. He felt there was no hope for her.

"She was never as strong as you. Something inside her was damaged and she thrived on magic and bad men, both of which pertained to me at the time. It took me many years to accept that her fate may have been destined even before we met."

"I didn't ask for any special powers. I never wanted to be bad." Kit's voice came out choked as if lumps formed in her throat as she tried to speak against the emotion welling up inside her. Pain and guilt struck him through their empathic blood bond.

"No, I know you didn't." He brushed a tear from the corner of her eye. "But I know you can find your humanity again. Once this is all over we'll find it together. If you lacked strength, we wouldn't be talking like this right now."

"You mean what we did could have changed me into some demon permanently?"

"Oh, little one. Even if both of us had our wish of normalcy I'm certain there would always be a little demon inside you."

A few hours remained until morning. He sat up and straddled Kit's body. She gave him a smile, pushing up against him. "I want another test."

Without much coaxing his nether region stirred back into action.

"We've only begun."

CHAPTER SEVEN

Kit sucked the sugar from the sweet sticks Mane propped next to her mouth before falling asleep. Hunger and exhaustion gnawed at her stomach after their all night romp, but she really only wanted to stay awake.

She kept chewing on the sweet stick, watching as the daylight crept through the window above their heads. Mane had said everything she ever hoped to hear from him last night. His love for her didn't change the fact that she needed to leave him behind. To protect him. There was no doubt she should be the one to face her mother, the selkie queen.

And she needed to do it alone.

Mane slept like someone with no worries on his mind. His rhythmic pattern of breathing almost lulled her into a false sense of security. Thank goodness the blood bond didn't allow him to read her mind.

From above a sliver of light cut across the ceiling, gradually widening as the light of day began to make its way across Underworld. Who knew how long she would have. Recently nights seemed to last twenty hours or more, leaving her precious little time to waste.

Light filled the chamber and the binds around her wrists and ankles loosened. Careful not to rock the bed she pulled herself free, easing her bare feet onto the copper tile floor. Mane's sword lay inches from his face on the nightstand. On tiptoes she easily sneaked the weapon into her satchel. Mane remained undisturbed. Hopefully he would understand she did this to protect him.

After putting on her glasses and amulet she grabbed a t-shirt and some boots and hurried outside. Her arms ached as she stretched them overhead, soaking in the morning sunlight. Her selkie scales formed into a shimmering pair of opalescent leggings. Even wounded, the forest's perfume with notes of oakmoss and balsam struck a chord, reminding her to hurry lest their song be cut short. She whipped the bandage off her hand and flung it to the ground. Only a thin red line remained.

Tracing the angry mark with her fingertip elicited a twinge of pleasure from her nether regions. Mane created a lust line right between the lines for her head and her heart. Sounded about right though completely unnecessary. He dialed into her inner soul the moment they met.

The position of the sun signaled mid-morning. Whatever spell had descended over the land also seemed to be affecting the amount of daylight. Precious little time remained to decide which direction to travel. She allowed her primal senses to pull her through the dense underbrush. Her selkie side sang out for water. With Mount Elbrus to her back she marched into the red-tinted forest.

After she had been hiking a short time a rattling sound from the brush froze her in place. Growing up near the canyons she knew that to be the warning call of a rattlesnake. She didn't have a clear line of sight. Panic momentarily seized her gut. She didn't dare take a deep breath to calm herself, instead letting the wash of adrenaline sharpen her senses. Clusters of cinnabar weighed down the trees surrounding her on all sides.

She picked up her feet and saw the bottoms of her shoes and legs were covered in red dust. She clutched the selkie amulet around her neck. Usually this much cinnabar turned any creature, demon or otherwise, into a raving madman. How had it all gotten here?

From the brush to her right erupted a strange animal. Its bird-like head, no taller than she, cocked to the side, studying the dagger in her hand. Another rattle emitted from the long serpentine tail it whipped back and forth. Two large wings beat the air furiously. At the end of two large feet were talons, much like the chicken feet her father used to prepare back home.

He loved those things. She hated them. And she hated this thing standing before her. A line of drool dripped from the side of its sharp beak and one bulging eye sized her up.

From the brush to its left, a small buckrabbit with unnaturally bright red eyes entered the clearing. The fuzzy bunny hissed, frozen in the creature's stare, then withered and disintegrated into a pile of cinnabar dust. The wind picked up, pulling the pile of red ash upward. The King was right. She should wear her glasses more often. A stabbing pain zipped from her hand into her head.

The mutant chicken took a step forward and opened its mouth, letting out a high-pitched screech. The ground under her feet started to crumble. She took the opportunity to run in the other direction, hoping the trench would create an obstacle. She had forgotten about the wings. The beast bounded over the ditch with one hop. The ground shook. Dry branches snapped as she brushed them aside. The creature closed in behind her. Where the hell was all the water? Hopefully this feathered vermin couldn't swim.

Another pealing wail rang from the depths of its hungry gut. Going vegetarian sounded good, if she lived long enough. Goosebumps broke out over her arms at the thought she might soon be a pile of buckrabbit dust. A giant tree appeared, offering sanctuary in its strong limbs. She cursed herself for leaving without Mane.

She swung up into the higher branches and froze, hiding until the perturbed poultry passed by.

She dared to glance over the edge, the rough bark biting into her palm and sending another sharp pain through her spine. The wounded limb groaned under her shifting weight. The creature's head swiveled straight up, locating its prey due to her stupidity. An electric green tongue and the scent of death slid out from the sharpened beak, red eyes glowing and likely confused as to why she remained in one piece.

One sharp talon dug into the tree and then another. True fear struck her to the core. It was coming for her and she was all alone with only a short sword.

❧❦

A searing pain traveled from Mane's hand up into his skull jolting him awake. In all his time with the elves the blood bond had never produced such a side effect. He pulled the wrappings off his hand and studied the thin red line. The scar looked normal, nothing unusual. A searing pain shot through his hand again throwing him onto his back. Lying in the plush bed he noticed two things. First, daylight flooded the room. The second, Kit and his sword were gone. He slipped his pants and shirt on then donned the helm. He grabbed Kit's whip left carelessly behind the dressing screen, the only other weapon on board. She had run off in a hurry if she forgot this. If anyone hurt Kit, no weapon would keep them safe.

He ran out of the ship and down the gangplank, letting the blood magic pull him toward her location. She had gone in the opposite direction of Mount Elbrus.

Damn you, Kit. Why did you go this way?

Mane pushed at their emotional connection and felt the walls she put up to hide from him. They weren't high enough. Through her stubborn will he felt her concern. Her fear. Despite not wanting to hurt him she made a poor decision. She better not die because he wanted to kill her. He sprinted through the trees, following Kit's tracks and the pull. Red, cinnabar-tinged sweat dripped from his brow. Only one beast generated such thick clouds of the stuff. He knew the owner of the second set of tracks stalking Kit.

A scream echoed out as he pushed the last of the brush away and came face to face with the basilisk. From the cradle of Acheron and sent, no doubt, by Ravanna to make a mess of this land and get everyone under his control. Unfortunately they traveled in packs.

He entered a clearing and saw Kit perched precariously in a tree. She held a sword in her hand, his sword, and was doing her best to stab at the talon of the basilisk. One hop and the beast would have her.

"Don't get too close or look into its eyes or it will turn you into a pile of dust," yelled Kit. Her glasses kept her safe. Something else kept him safe. Great, another "secret" to explain to her. He didn't want to have to tell Kit how deep his connection ran with Acheron and Ravanna.

But she would know soon enough.

Like an old-fashioned shoot out, he and the basilisk squared off. Kit cried out as he got closer. "No, Mane, please. You need to save yourself, please."

"Don't worry. The basilisk can't hurt me."

A long time had passed since he'd seen one of these creatures. They were a weapon of old, but considering the amount of dust in the forest, they were doing their job. The basilisk destroyed everything in its wake. The cinnabar left behind transformed any living soul into a slave for Ravanna. The reality of Mane's fears stood before him, a silent battle cry echoing in his ears from many millennia ago, age old weapons for an age old battle Ravanna never stopped fighting.

He leaned down, closed his hand around the foot of the basilisk and gave a sharp tug. A mass of feathers and sharp squalls of pain dropped to his feet. As expected the submissive animal bowed before him. "Pass me my sword."

"But why doesn't it try attacking you?" Kit tossed down the sword and he caught the hilt one-handed. The basilisk squalled as he put the tip of the blade under its chin.

"I am second in command of Acheron. The only other rank higher is the demon King himself. And he isn't here right now. I know because if Ravanna were here the basilisk would attack."

"Well, now I don't feel like such a badass. You get the crown. Thanks for the newsflash. How did you know Ravanna wasn't here in Underworld when you came over here?" Kit kept her smart mouth and herself in the tree.

"I didn't. But I can't let you die." Mane stared at the hapless creature. "You tell Ravanna he can't have the Realms. He sent me here and now I have a responsibility. I will fight to protect these people."

The basilisk gave out a sharp cry and bowed his head, retreating into the brush.

Kit dropped down to the ground and ran over, putting her hands around his neck. "Why did you let it go?"

"Because the only way I can get a message to Ravanna down in Acheron is through that basilisk. I am not allowed there in body or voice."

Halfway through the brush the basilisk stopped and let loose the telltale rattle from a twitching tail. A sure sign of attack.

"Get back up in the tree." One hand on the dagger and the other on the whip, adrenaline shot through his veins.

Kit hesitated. "What?"

"Get. Back. In. The. Tree. Now!" He flung Kit to the side as the beast barreled straight for him. He swung his sword up then brought down the blade between the basilisk's shoulders. The huge carcass dissolved instantly into a pile of red ash. Mane lost his balance and tumbled to the ground. A swift wind blew away all remaining evidence.

Kit ran over and helped him to his feet. Damn ash would probably stick in his hair for weeks.

"I thought you said it wouldn't attack you."

"I said it wouldn't attack me as long as Ravanna remained in Acheron. Things just got worse."

CHAPTER EIGHT

Kit clung to Mane, concentrating on the rise and fall of his chest. *In and out*, each breath measuring what might be their last seconds together. Religion had never brought her comfort, but it was funny how prayer seemed appropriate right about now.

Her father sometimes took her to church service but only in his desperation to find a cure for her illness. Faith healers couldn't help her. An exorcism might have done more harm than good. Expel the demon and part of her would go too. Last night Mane forced her to surrender to the possession and with his help she won. Their remaining problems now resided somewhere out there in the Riparian and at the bottom of Lake Mavrovo.

"We have to split up. Ravanna is your big bad and my mother is mine. There isn't any other way." Mane squeezed her tighter. If breathing became necessary she would have a problem. Therein lay the dilemma. Mane had to breathe. He couldn't come into the waters of Mavrovo.

"No. Promise me now you won't sneak away from me again." Mane tucked a lock of hair behind her ear.

Having them together might not be a good idea, but she couldn't imagine ever leaving his side. Even without the blood bond, the thought of splitting up from Mane tore at her heart. There had to be a way. "I won't. I promise."

"Good." Mane took the sword and tucked the deadly steel into the scabbard at his waist. "Because if you do I will withhold pleasure from you for a week."

"Like you'd last that long." Kit hurried to keep pace with Mane's long strides as they headed deeper into the Riparian. Every time the dead leaves crunched under her boots she cringed. The empty forest echoed their every movement, betraying them to Ravanna.

Mane smirked, a familiar and welcome smile coming across his face. "Ravanna has drawn enough power to open a portal and squeeze himself through. Mavrovo seems the most likely place."

"Yes, but you can't follow me down unless you have a magic pair of gills I don't know about."

"You've seen every part of me. Good and bad." Mane lifted his chin, exposing his neck. Warmth flooded between her thighs. "No gills but I do have help from our friend Dooley." He pulled a little blue pill out of his satchel.

"Did he have a good laugh when he gave that to you?"

"Is this another reference to something human I don't know about?" Mane rolled the pill between his fingers. Despite the aching buds of her nipples, she clamped a hand over her mouth to stifle her laughter. Mane impotent would be hell incarnate. The wound on her hand brushed against her teeth and a sizzle of pain zapped into her wrist.

Mane took her hand gently in his and turned her palm. A white hot need blossomed from her core at his gentle touch and hard stare.

"Let me see." He examined the wound before retrieving

a tub of ointment. "Along with more of this, Dooley gave me a pill that allows me to follow you down into Mavrovo."

"Dooley really knows what he's doing."

Mane grunted and shoved the salve into his bag. "Let's get moving. Daylight is short now and I want to make it to Mavrovo before it gets dark."

"Wait." Kit caught Mane's wrist as he turned away. "You're not actually acting jealous are you?"

"What do you expect, Kit? I did find you on top of him in the hallway."

"That was before I learned how to control myself. I'm good now. We're good now." She held this moment in her hands like a child marveling at the delicate tableau within a snow globe. Mane gave her the gift of independence – but it was fragile. Inside the white particles churned up a violent storm contained by a transparent glass shield. Frozen in this moment, the dust settling ever so slowly, the scene became clear. With a full heart and the man in front of her to thank, she sank down to her knees and worked to undo the clasp on Mane's belt. There was definitely one way to show him his lesson had been assimilated.

The tension in Mane's thighs melted away underneath her grip. "Practice makes perfect." His fingers lingered on her cheek before his knees loosened and the tree at his back became necessary to hold him upright.

She could definitely learn a predilection for this delicacy over the usual meal she sank her teeth into. Her own thighs quivered as she savored the exposed ridge along his hardened shaft. Their moans echoed through the forest. Kit dipped a finger into her swollen folds, coming right to the edge. It was time to just let go and trust that things would work out. Freedom from all the binds holding each part of her in check. Permission to enjoy each moment, including this one, more fully.

Mane's peak thundered through their blood bond, rocking her onto her heels. The feast was over. She slid her fingers down her belly into the glistening cream, letting them dance over the enflamed spot between her legs until she crossed the boundary into her own pleasure.

Mane thrust his chest out, hooking his thumbs into his belt loops to tug his pants into place. A knowing grin spread across his face. "I knew you could do it."

"Have you forgotten all those other times?"

"Yes, but your eyes have never remained human before."

❧

Mane could barely contain his pride. He knew Kit was capable of so much more than she gave herself credit for. His lungs expanded to their fullest through deep, contented breaths. Hope lay beneath the rotten puffs of cinnabar loam lacing the land. The air held the crisp scent of fertile soil deep within the brooding forest — life ready to bloom once freed. But nature wasn't the only thing lurking in the landscape. A face stared out at him, barely discernible but very familiar.

Kit's eyes narrowed, confusion at what she obviously scented.

Feigning chivalry he bent down to whisper in Kit's ear. "It's my brother Torkel. Give us a moment alone."

"You can't be serious. He's already tried to kill you once." Kit's hand slipped through thin air at her waist, expecting to find the coiled snake whip which he carried on his belt. He handed the whip to her without letting go. "Let me take care of this."

"You'll have your chance. This is not your battle." His

grip on Kit's wrist loosened as she pulled away, tucking the whip at her side and nodding with understanding. If she expected to handle her mother without his interference she needed to let him handle Torkel on his own.

"I'm going to clean myself up really quick." She clapped her hands together and hopped to her feet then disappeared into the nearby brush.

"You lie with the selkie whore who killed one of our own? For a moment I regretted having to kill you. Thank you, this makes it so much easier." Mane wheeled around to see Torkel, his elven brother, standing about fifty feet away, an arrow held taut in his bow. Elven archers were deadly accurate.

Torkel's mossy green cloak hung in tatters about his frail frame. It killed Mane to see Torkel looking in such desolate shape, though he knew he would have to face him at some point. The Riparian usually sustained the elves but Ravanna's meddling took away that livelihood. Mane raised his arms. "I'm not here to threaten your position amongst the elves."

A rustling in the underbrush distracted him for a moment, enough time for Torkel to let his arrow loose. The stone head sank into the flesh of Mane's upper arm, stopping as it hit bone. Torkel lunged forward and shoved the bow into Mane's gut, knocking him off balance. They tumbled to the ground, Torkel's bony knees pinning Mane's shoulders to the ground.

"Get off me, Torkel, and I may let you live." Mane struggled under Torkel's desperate grip and tried not to think about how much damage he had inadvertently caused the elves by being reborn as one of their own.

Torkel leaned into the arrow, driving it deeper into his shoulder. "You don't seem to realize our position here, brother. I sank an arrow into you. You are beneath me. I hold the position of power. Here and at our tribe. You know our laws won't allow you to give your position to me. As long as you live you hold title."

If Torkel killed him Ravanna would probably put him right back, stealing the soul of another innocent elven child to continue his imprisonment of Mane's soul. "I appreciate your enthusiasm for my demise, but you'll have to get in line. I believe Ravanna is first."

Torkel rolled off Mane and took a few steps backward. "You lie. Ravanna can't be here, it's impossible." The shock on Torkel's face was obvious. Hunger must have made him delusional. No one could miss what was happening.

"Are you stupid or blind or both?" Mane ripped the arrow from his arm and threw the broken shaft to the ground. The gaping hole left behind hurt like hell, but letting Torkel know he got in a good shot wouldn't help matters. Mane took a handful of the cinnabar dust lacing the ground and rubbed the poultice into his arm. The mineral sank in, knitting him closed from the inside out. A few more passes erased almost all evidence of the wound.

"The red sand is poison. You're playing devil's games." All the color in Torkel's face faded, but he stood his ground, ego trumping fear. A good thing because the elven tribe needed a strong leader in the dark days to come and Mane was hoping Torkel would be their champion.

"You've always known I am not like you. Father knew as well. I can't take your position. I am not a true elf. I am of Acheron."

"Demon!" Torkel nocked another arrow.

"Save your ammunition for the real enemy. You've seen my ability to heal."

"Not from a shot straight through the heart. I won't miss next time."

"I don't suspect you would." He sidestepped, trying to position himself out of Torkel's line of fire. A shot to the heart would be more than anyone could survive. His brother mirrored his movements. "I am here to help stop this red sand from destroying everything. Please, return to the elves. Take them to Dell'Aria. King Delos will protect you. The Riparian isn't safe for you anymore."

"The elves are not cowards, Mane. We don't run like you did. We fight."

"Think of your mother, Torkel. She's already lost one son. Don't make her lose her other son too. You can be a good leader for our people."

"Dear Goddess." Torkel's arrow dropped from his trembling hand, his face gone ashen.

Kit appeared from the brush, her anger rolling through their blood bond like a tsunami, a rapidly rising tide about to flatten his elven brother.

"I wonder if you taste as good as your brother did." Kit focused eyes as black as coal on her target, catching him in her mesmerizing gaze. Kit's selkie magic rained a terrorizing blind rage upon Torkel, an unseen powerful force that tore even further into his damaged psyche, destroying the confident elven leader he tried to build up.

"Run, Torkel," Mane said. "Tell the tribe to escape the forest. Contact the King and don't return until enough time has passed for this land to heal itself." Torkel didn't take much more encouragement. He'd witnessed Kit's speed first hand.

"Give him a sporting chance, I get it. I'll give him a minute. I was wondering what was on the menu today. Dilemma solved." Kit took a deep inhale, whip in hand. The thong uncoiled and the scent of freshly oiled leather ripened his awareness. The huntress was in full force. Good for later, but not now.

"No, Kit. He has a destiny to fulfill." He hated leaving Torkel to run free in the Riparian, but the elves would wait for their leader to return. If he didn't return they wouldn't leave. Their safety would be at risk. The only mother he'd known and true friends were mixed alongside those like Torkel and he wouldn't directly be involved in their demise. Guilt struck him hard. The true fate of these people lay in his hands now, his and Kit's. Hopefully they would both be able to do the right thing.

"He's no better than Kali. Every time I see him he's causing trouble. You can't trust him, Mane, and if you let him live, you'll regret it." Kit spoke through her sharpened fangs with forced restraint.

"My brother. My risk." He placed a hand on Kit's shoulder and a tremor passed through her body, tension releasing at his touch. She took a deep breath and the darkness faded from her eyes.

Kit examined what was left of the wound at his shoulder. "Seems I really can't leave you alone. You'll have use for that little blue pill after all."

"The sooner we both accept our roles the faster we can end this."

❧

A purplish pink haze filled the sky above the shores of Mavrovo. Day would soon become night. The point of no return right at the tips of her toes, lapping at the shore.

Kit had seen the lake from her perch up high in Dell'Aria. Up close its burbling red surface churned with cinnabar dust that turned the water thick as molasses. Selkie lived underwater, but breathing this stuff seemed out of the question.

At the edge of the shore stood the tree of her earlier temptations, once laden with luscious fruit on the day she met Mane. Now its branches sagged heavily, the roots surrounded in viscous red muck, dark magic robbing the life from its veins like the selkie sleep which took her youth.

"What now?" Stopping her mother appeared unrealistic. So much damage already done.

"We go to the Queen and agree to join her army. Tell her you're finally ready to lead the selkie out of the waters of Mavrovo to walk the Underworld."

"Talk to her, yes, but she'll never believe I want to join her. We're not exactly best buds." The memory of her first meeting with her mother twirled around her soul, tighter than the lock of blue hair around her index finger. One touch from Elemi on this shore had ignited her latent selkie spirit and, for better or worse, she'd never been the same since. She couldn't deny her mother's caress and the waters of Mavrovo saved her life.

Mane hung his satchel in their tree, testing the branch to make sure it would accept the weight without breaking. His helm and all his clothes save his loincloth were stowed away inside. "You need to find a way to convince her. The selkie and their Queen will be weakest on land. We can't fight them underwater. If she knows what Ravanna has planned, then up here is where I can make her talk. Your mother and your people are all pawns in his game. The Queen should know the pawns always get sacrificed first. I can wait outside the castle, make sure nothing takes you by surprise while you talk to her."

Games of strategy were never Kit's strong suit. A chess player had to plan several moves ahead. "How long can you be under?"

Mane dropped the pill into his mouth. "Dooley wasn't

certain. We'll have to be quick."

"Good thing my father taught me a mean game of poker." Kit swept the mask of doubt from her face and stepped into the red water. A familiar spark raced across its surface. If Elemi didn't already know they were here, she knew now.

Kit didn't fight her natural inclination to let her selkie side take over. In the water's reflection her eyes went black, teeth extended. Her humanity had to be sacrificed for this mission.

"Together." She held Mane's hand and dove down.

The amulet worked its magic as soon as she entered the water, pulling her and Mane towards its rightful owner. Queen Elemi. She let the current take them down. Thoughts of what she would say to Mom flitted through her mind. *Hi, Mom, long time no see. Yeah, about that selkie prophecy you always wanted me to fulfill, I'm ready to do that now. Let's get to it.*

An undertow snuck up on them and pulled Mane in the opposite direction. It only took a split second for a ruddy cloud to swallow him whole. Panic struck her core. The amulet continued to pull down, the heavy chain digging into the soft flesh of her neck. She wanted to scream out for Mane so he could find her, but her voice stuck behind the noose of her amulet.

The strength of the magic increased in the deeper regions of the lake, pulling her faster toward the bottom. Further away from Mane. A host of stragglers followed in her wake. Bulbous lusca, half-octopus and half-shark, their tentacles floating behind them. Swollen sea serpents, mouths agape with rows of ivory incisors. Amongst them all the Charybdis with its tunnel of teeth capable of swallowing several elves at once.

Selkie armies easily kept the other inhabitants of

Mavrovo at bay, but she was alone. Fighting all these creatures at once would be impossible. The snare tightened. Mane was gone and this damn magic was stealing from her again. First her life and now her love. She wedged her fingers under the chain, unable to stop her momentum and the agonizing scream that ripped from her mouth as the metal lace snapped and lashed against her palm. Fresh blood poured from the open wound.

Anticipating attack she swung around and drew the whip from the belt at her side, but strangely the creatures appeared blind to her presence. Their bloated bodies slowed and bumped against one another before floating away. *Dead.* She should have expected it. The cinnabar had killed everything in Underworld, why not affect Mavrovo?

Free of her neck, the amulet shot away. Now all alone, her only comfort came from the blood bond connecting her to Mane. If something were wrong she would feel it.

"Mane, can you hear me?" Bubbles sprang forth as she called out. Selkie could speak under water, but sound didn't travel as far as on land. He had to be nearby. A hand shot out from the gloom to her right. Greenish-gold scales traveled from the tips of the fingers clamped around her wrist and up to the head of one of the selkie guard. Annoying but hardly shocking. Living in Mavrovo made her numb to these brutish nannies.

"Took you long enough, but you need to stop. I didn't come here alone." She didn't want to mention Mane, but leaving him behind wasn't an option either. The guard wouldn't even look in her direction, merely continued mindlessly on his task to bring her back to her mother. Soon the castle spires would come into view. The next move was hers. Cold, stiff fingers clamped down harder on her wrist. "If you hold me any tighter you'll probably be taking just my hand to the Queen."

Adrenaline spiked through her cortex. There wasn't any explanation for the way her heart raced or her muscles tensed except for fear. Pure, unadulterated fear that didn't originate from her.

Mane appeared through the blood-red haze on her left, a look of panic of his face, his hands reaching toward her. She waited for the sense of relief to flood through her mind. They had found one another.

Instead she watched as Mane drew the sword from his belt and yelled at the guard. "Stop!"

If she didn't convince this guard to get his meat hooks off her there would be blood shed before they could even reach her mother. Pulling rank topped the list of her most hated activities. Before letting loose her command she drew her eyebrows together in the best scowl she could manage.

"Your princess demands you to stop, asshole." The selkie guard jerked to a halt, turning to face her. The usual visage of the selkie terrified most –blackened eyes, razor sharp teeth, faces elongated just enough to seem alien and frightening to any denizen of the Realms. Perversely nightmarish creatures with powers to mesmerize their prey, stunning them into complacency while they tore their heads off.

This was worse.

ॐ

Mane cursed himself for being so stupid. Fae, like the one in the King's chambers, weren't the only beings affected by Ravanna's poison red dust. To truly control the selkie Ravanna turned them into his own army, the army of the undead.

Pushing the zombified selkie off Kit didn't take much

effort. Individually it was weak. Unfortunately the sentinel now knew fresh meat filled the water and with an unknown signal they were rapidly surrounded. Back to back with Kit, he weighed their options.

"Don't worry. They may be out of their mind, but with the Queen's amulet around your neck they won't attack. I'm sure of it." Despite his words Mane drew the sword hanging at his waist and looked for a crack in the herd.

"There's one problem with that theory. I let the necklace go."

A keening chorus of moans collectively rose from the selkie, the whites of their eyes glowing through the darkness. He couldn't stop staring into their empty eyes.

"Remind me again what your kind does before they attack." They continued to revolve in a circle, the noose of hungry cadaverous creatures tightening.

Kit pulled the whip from her side and snapped the braided leather forward, striking the arm of a nearby zombie. The limb separated at the elbow and floated into the water. Hollow eyes looked at the remaining stump and continued its forward progress, only mildly perturbed. "Usually we move too fast for there to be any warning. I think these things are moving at their top speed."

The slow crush pushed in close enough for him to take a swipe at one's head which severed with ease, drifting into the fray. The obvious attack agitated the front line and suddenly they were besieged with snapping teeth. Mindless mouths searched out any square inch of flesh. Kit lashed out with the only weapon she had. The whip took out several beasts at once but they were quickly becoming overwhelmed. The thong of the whip became entangled in the mass of flesh, ripping her only weapon from her hands.

A faint light shone through the gloom. "Kit, over there!"

Pointing out the beacon gave his assailant the perfect opportunity to attack. Sharp incisors bit into his arm and ripped to the side, taking along a measure of his flesh. Easy as stripping roasted chicken from the bone. His sword fell from his hands. Blood flowed into the water from his open wound and mixed with the cinnabar brew causing an explosion of excitement amongst the zombies. Although his flesh was beginning to reknit itself, the cocktail had already been served. An acute sense of purpose heightened his senses and sharpened his focus. Even half dead the selkie knew what they craved. Demon Delight would be the main course followed by Kit Kabobs for dessert if they couldn't get out of there.

He pulled Kit toward the light. "Hurry, the castle can't be far. Swim." Two legs were nothing compared to the swift fins of all the selkie closing in behind them. Too much blood in the water. Too much cinnabar. If they didn't increase the distance soon they would be overrun.

He clasped his strong arm around Kit's waist and held fast as she beat a furious pace through the water. The space between them and the slower moving zombies increased.

Blackened spires came into view sitting atop wrought iron towers. Mystical flames danced within lanterns around the perimeter of the selkie Queen's lair. Clumps of neon widgeon grass signaled their arrival at the lake bottom.

The castle gate stood before them. A false moat surrounded the footings — a bottomless crevasse reputed to run deeper than the pathways to Acheron. The only thing standing between them and safety. He knew what the realm of the demon King held. If anything worse resided in the greatest depths of Mavrovo he never wanted to find out.

With only a quick glance down, they reached the gate, Kit's hand in his. "Are you ready for this?" she asked.

He didn't expect to have to enter the castle with Kit, but plans change. Now they both would face Queen Elemi and he wasn't exactly on her good side.

"Yes, hurry." The swell had caught up with them, following the thin bloody trail from his arm.

A familiar wailing sounded above their heads as he closed his fingers around the door handle. From the murder holes set within the gate towers, a second wave of selkie poured forth. A storm of gaping maws rained down, jaws unhinging as if to swallow them whole.

One yank on the handle and the barrier between them and refuge didn't budge. Kit pressed her body into his as the herd following them gathered at the edge of the crevasse. Kit had lost her weapon too. They were pinned between a closed door and a standing wave of opposition which could only end in their demise.

Heart thrashing in his chest he continued to tug at the door. If they were on land he could pound the damn thing down, but muscle power didn't matter much in the water. Here he was weightless and hopeless, but ever determined.

A blanket of hungry mouths descended, blocking out all light. He held Kit tighter. With every last breath he would fight these monsters, shield Kit from the rending they were about to receive. Maybe she could get away if they were focused on him.

Before he could act, tickling tendrils snaked up his legs and a wall of bubbles erupted from the crevasse. A giant red plume shot up to his right, barreling through their attackers. Vibrations filled his limbs spiking shockwaves of pain through his ruined forearm. Shrieks echoed through the water. Bodies swirled around them.

Kit's fingers dug deeper into his side. A vortex erupted from the crevasse. At the center of the swirling black mass a dark spot burned. An eye. The portal to Acheron. Mane held tight to the door. He'd rather they both die here than be dragged into Ravanna's realm.

"Hold tight." Kit hoisted herself over his shoulder and put her hand on the door. A pulse of blue light shimmered and the door swung inward, sucking them inside and depositing them onto the cool marble floor. The door clanged shut behind them.

"Next time maybe you'll remember ladies go first."

Right, selkie magic opens selkie doors. Despite being hundreds of years older than Kit she still had a lot to teach him.

❧

They were safe for the moment, Kit told herself, but she shivered as the gate closed and the rumbling under their feet came to a halt. Outside these walls the world was deteriorating. Within, every surface gleamed – no magic lost here. Crystalline waters were unaffected by the plague outside.

Mane leaned against a gilded bench usually reserved for the Queen's Guard. "I think I'll stay here if you don't mind," he said.

Mane's normally tan skin was pallid as he sank down onto the seat, his back sliding down the wall. The fight with the selkie had cut Mane's time short. As much as she wanted to linger in the great hall, the time for procrastination was over. "I'll be quick."

Each step down the long corridor brought Kit closer to the door to her mother's chambers. The last time they met, Elemi had been conspiring with Ravanna. Whatever was about to happen between them would be her mother's fault. Elemi deserved punishment.

She eased the door open, the weak mantra on a continuous loop in her mind.

A lantern on her mother's bureau, aflame with an enchanted fire, highlighted the outline of a body underneath the bedcovers. The only other source of light in the room was the blue glow of Elemi's amulet, the one she had gifted to her daughter, the one she'd lost in the ocean. It had returned to Elemi.

Kit started and backed quickly against the rough stone of the opposite wall at the sight of her mother's withered hand that clasped the amulet. The coward in her wanted to hide under the bed, but she was no longer a child so she waited for the fingers to flex, show any sign of movement, scared to death her mother would wake up and scared she wouldn't.

Forever seemed to pass. Mane's death would be on her hands if she couldn't work up the courage to question her mother about Ravanna. This wallflower was going to find a dance partner no matter how uncoordinated she felt. On top of the bureau a weathered volume lay open, the ornate language of a spell gracing the page. It didn't take a degree in Shakespearean prose to know this was a spell meant to allow the selkie, all of them, to walk outside the waters of Mavrovo.

"I wouldn't have had to do it at all if you had come back sooner." Elemi's voice barely rose above a whisper. Only a fool would assume a selkie weak. They were experts in seducing trust to gain a treasure, usually in the form of an open vein. Disguise and trickery were mainstays of her people. *The only way you got what you wanted.* The white satin covers drifted to the side and Elemi sat up, leaving her face in the shadows.

A sense of self-preservation kicked in and Kit's back

hugged the wall. "You know I never wanted to help you destroy the Realms."

"And yet you already have." Elemi choked and gasped, like a fish flopping on dry land.

"I've come here to stop you, not to help you. It seems you already did my job for me. Everyone is dead. I assume that was your doing." She found her strength returning. Now to figure out what her mother did and reverse the process. If she could do that then she could get her and Mane out of there. "What happened? How did you let Ravanna through? How did you open the portal?"

"He tricked me." The shadows dropped down from Elemi's face as she leaned forward. The light from the amulet reflected the damage to her mother's previously regal visage. Cheeks sunken and arms thin and frail, she pointed at the book of spells. "That spell. I've always knew it to be a part of the selkie legacy. Something we were supposed to work toward. A leader, not of us, who would bring the selkie out of these dark depths and into the light."

Elemi choked again and a wash of red flooded from her mouth into the surrounding waters.

"What's wrong?" Elemi's distress seemed real, not a trick, and suddenly concern for the dying soul before her replaced the fear of her mother. She sat next to Elemi and placed a hand on her back.

Elemi wrapped skeletal arms around herself as if trying to hold herself together. "I'm drowning. Slowly. Drowning. Like all the rest."

"They all drowned?" Her explanation, while sounding farfetched, made sense. There were no signs of struggle. "They had no idea what was happening to them. Beings that lived and breathed underwater suddenly given the ability to breathe air and they had no idea what to do. I remember how foreign each breath of the waters of Mavrovo once felt. How could you do that to your own people? Each breath that once gave them life is now giving them death and robbing them of their ability to fight, the darkness engulfing them until the waters take from them all it has ever given, turning them into Ravanna's army of the undead."

Elemi answered with a small nod.

She thumbed through the book. As she touched the pages containing the words to the spell her mother cast, they disintegrated. The whole thing had been an illusion. The roiling heat of betrayal filled her belly.

"I thought you were the key," Elemi said. "I thought you were supposed to lead us out. He tricked me. He used me. Now he has all the selkie deaths on his hands and enough magic to keep the portal between our worlds open indefinitely."

Kit didn't know much about magic, but she learned growing up that you could find the answer to any question within a book. Books were her friends when she had none and they opened doors to worlds she thought she would never get to see, including her own.

Now she hoped this book would give her the answer on how to close the doors between the worlds.

"Mom, you're alive." She paused and looked into her mother's black eyes. Eyes like hers. "How are you alive?"

"I don't know. But there can really only be one answer."

As much as she usually avoided spoilers, Kit flipped to the end of the tome. The second to last page held all the answers. None of which she wanted to face.

CHAPTER NINE

Every breath provided less oxygen. If Mane didn't get out of the water soon he would lose everything. His immortal life would remain intact, but he could lose this body and all his memories. Memories of Kit. Ravanna would delight in sending him back into the form of some other newborn babe to start all over again. Of course the memories of Catherine would remain to torture him. The painful thought was equal only to the sharp ache filling his lungs.

Kit appeared at the end of the hall with a book under her right arm, half hidden in the doorframe, her movements precise. Shoulders pushed back, she exuded the calm and focus of someone determined to complete the task set before them. The amulet hung around her neck and a new sword was tucked in her waistband. Hopefully her mother gave them what they needed. However, any ritual to close the portal would have to wait. They needed to get out of there now.

Kit took another step and he saw Elemi under her other arm. The once powerful selkie Queen drooped heavily to the side. Her pallor suggested an imminent death, like the fate of her people. His heart went out to Kit.

"We need to get you both up top before you drown."

"She's drowning too?" Drowning was not something you usually thought of with creatures that spent their lives underwater.

"Same as you, hot shot." Elemi coughed and Kit struggled to keep her upright.

He looked down at his own hands. Sure enough, his nails were bluish-gray, reflective of the low oxygen level in his blood. "I don't know how much help I can be."

"You won't need to. I can get Elemi to the surface and protect myself." Kit patted the weapon at her side and set the book down before opening a closet off the hallway. She brought out a pair of wings, except instead of being covered in feathers they were more akin to those of a dragon. A thin membrane stretched across finger-like joints. "Get to open water and place your arms through these loops. You'll be up top in no time." Her smile wavered underneath the forced enthusiasm. A sound plan that meant they had to separate again.

He took the wings, noticing the empty closet. "How about you?"

"Last pair. The others must have tried to use them once they realized what was happening. I don't know. You need it more. I can get my mother topside. I'll just take a little longer. You don't have a little longer."

He hated to admit she was right. However, if he wanted to be around to protect her in the future he had to save himself now. He eased the gate open and peered outside. The activity had stopped. The selkie were nowhere to be found.

"I'll see you soon." He ignored the look of death Elemi

directed toward him and brought Kit in for a short embrace.

"Yes, you will see me soon. Hurry."

A few feet away from the castle he slipped his arms through the loops. Jet-like forces propelled him upward. His lungs constricted and stars dotted his eyes. He'd been through a lot of pain and torture but this feeling took things to a new level. He fought to stay aware while focusing on the dot of light in the near distance, longing for sweet air almost as much as he yearned for Kit. Despite his will, his rapid ascent and oxygen starved body lost the fight.

Terror filled his heart before darkness clouded his vision.

Seconds or hours had passed, he was uncertain which. Someone watched him. Even without opening his eyes he felt the intensity, the hate. Had he survived Mavrovo only to perish by the hands of his enemy?

"Wake up. I can't properly destroy you when you're passed out." The voice of his former boss. Ravanna, the demon king.

Eyes half open he tried not to flinch at the sight of Ravanna's distinct purplish skin. Fear was the catalyzing agent to this whole showdown. He wouldn't win in his weakened state but he could buy some time for Kit.

"I would say it's good to see you, but I would be lying." He pushed himself up and stood tall in the presence of Ravanna, trying to hide the shaking in his oxygen-starved limbs. The cinnabar-infused waters at his feet weren't doing much to help him restore his energy. Things were worse than he thought.

"Mane, when will you ever learn? I took one play thing away, and I'll take your new one too." Ravanna's deep eggplant skin lightened to a brilliant shade of heliotrope as he backed into the waters and fed himself from the energy of the cinnabar.

Mane's eyes darted around the shore. There was no telling how long he had been out, but Kit was nowhere to be seen. "The rightful owner will always possess what is his even when it may not physically be within his grasp." His elven father told him he was different than the other demons of Acheron and that belief was finally starting to take hold.

"Keep telling yourself that. Cloak, now." Ravanna snapped his fingers and from behind the tree, the one he had shared with Kit, the one where he first saw his love stretch out on her tiptoes, came the one who most made his heart ache.

Catherine.

Her once silken auburn tresses were covered in soot and mire, collected together like some woebegone dreadlocks that should have been cut off long ago to spare their owner the burden. Her spine bowed under the weight of Ravanna's oppression, and pain etched her raddled face. A soiled white gown barely disguised the lead cuffs around her ankles.

He winced at every step she took, his own arms dropping to his sides. He wanted to escape this scene. It couldn't be real. An exquisite pain blossomed at the back of his throat. He replayed their last moments in his head, wishing there was something he could have done to change what happened, something he could do now.

"Cat." His former lover's nickname on his lips and suddenly out of his mouth was like taking in a breath and breathing it out again.

She blindly sought the source of the sound, searching the ether in front of her as if she viewed him through a fog. But her focus never settled. She couldn't see him.

Ravanna took a few steps toward Catherine and grabbed the cloak from her hands. As he did Mane saw the telltale bulge in reality. Catherine wasn't really there. She was trapped on the other side.

"You keep her like an animal." The rage inside his voice could not be hidden. For years he believed once Ravanna took Catherine, she would be dead. Nothing in his experience would have told him otherwise. As an assassin for Ravanna, he knew that was his favorite way to dispatch those who crossed him Earthside. Guilt hit him harder than Torkel's arrow.

"Yes. I do. You see, I figured I would need to keep her around since killing you is out and you might, at some point, need some motivation."

"But how?" He took a few steps toward the image of Catherine who stood and looked forward at nothing, her image flickering somewhere in another space and time.

"Those chains around her ankles? Keeps her tethered somewhat to the Earthside plain of existence. Enough so she is kept alive. She isn't spared the madness though. Believe me that has been extra fun all these years."

Hatred tempered with steely determination overcame him and he lunged at Ravanna, sending him stumbling into the shallow sludge of cinnabar runoff. Rolling around in the mire he reached for Ravanna's throat and held him under, pushing him down and bringing him up again.

In between he could hear the laughter of Ravanna in his ears. Gritting his teeth, he stopped and pushed himself back, leaving Ravanna to sit up again. He needed every ounce of strength to end this and Ravanna was successfully baiting him. No matter how much he wanted to, he couldn't possibly squeeze the life from Ravanna, but he might be able to prevent him from doing any more damage right now.

"You've been living this life too long. You seem to forget you can't kill me. You may have some power, but

you'll never succeed. Not on this plain or any other."
Ravanna stood and pulled his cloak, now dripping wet, from
the water. "And did you have to ruin my cloak? Now I have
to send Catherine to fetch another."

With the flick of his wrist Catherine shuffled off, the
lead weights clicking together, each clang making his insides
cringe. "No." He reached out and his hand passed through
her image. Only an apparition. His Catherine. Someday he
would find a way to free her. Now he would be lucky to get
out with his own life and memory intact.

"You won't be able to take the Realms, Ravanna. There
are too many here who will fight against you."

"You really have become stupid since you've been here,
Mane. Stupid and weak. How do you think I ended up here?
What do you think opened the portal between Acheron and
the Realms? Here, let me help you figure it out."

Ravanna grabbed his neck and shoved him down into
the waters of Mavrovo. Mane struggled in the shallow pool
but looked around for whatever Ravanna wanted him to see.
Perhaps the Demon King's ego would somehow work to his
advantage. He could see nothing but the red muck of the
cinnabar.

Ravanna pulled his head up. "Have you figured it out
yet? No? Keep working on it." He pushed his head down
again and Mane struggled to hold his breath, lungs on fire.
There was nothing more he wanted to do other than to take
a breath. He struggled against Ravanna's hold, unable to
fight back against his grip. His mouth opened involuntarily
and he breathed an ocean into his lungs. The cinnabar dulled
the pain momentarily. Then he breathed in the essence of all
those lost souls.

The water wasn't just full of cinnabar and the zombified
selkie fae. It was full of the dead. And they numbered in the

thousands. Ravanna yanked him back to the surface.

He choked on the sour brew, spitting it to the ground before taking in a deep breath of the sweet air. He never thought being alive would feel so good. Being alive. It was what he wanted more than anything else. To have a true heart beat inside his chest. To nestle against the one he loved within the span of a normal life. Normal.

"Have you figured it out yet?" Ravanna looked down upon him, arms crossed.

And he had. Finally figured out what he wanted. "Yes."

"Wonderful. So you'll leave now so I can do what I need to do. There is nothing you can do to stop me from taking over the rest of this world."

His father's words on the hunt came back to him. "Wherever you are, be all there. Don't just be there physically. Be there mentally as well. When you are trying to shoot your target, don't think about how the victory will taste. Forget about the past and don't think about the future. Focus on the task at hand."

Ravanna was who he was meant to fight. Through all his time in the Realms and elsewhere he had never felt such a hunger to destroy someone. "Act, don't think, the mind makes you nervous." Without any weapon but his faith he ran toward Ravanna, knocking into him with all the strength of a thousand men.

Ravanna rolled along with him and stood, holding him under the chin and pushing him up into the air as if he weighed nothing more than a small child. Ravanna pressed his body flush against the trunk of a tree, their tree, and quickly lashed him in place. Suspended upright, his foot could just skim the surface of the water below.

Rope wrapped from his ankles to his shoulders and kept him from making the slightest movement. Ravanna took a seat on a large boulder near the shore. He beckoned something forth from the deadened grasses on the shoreline. Several large basilisks slid out from the shadows, bowing their heads to their master and letting out a long slow hiss of cinnabar dust.

"Are you ready? I hope you like your seat for the main event. Your toy will be coming up soon. I will enjoy watching her as you die. It will be easier to break her once she is already broken."

Mane looked down into the waters below and tried to keep himself from smiling. The answer to his problems was right at his feet. His satchel must have fallen when Ravanna strung him up in the tree. A plan formed in his mind. He battled against his binds and the tree cracked and groaned under his struggles. He counted on its weakened strength to break under his greater weight. Without his hands free he would fall face first into the waters and drown. Likely exactly what Ravanna intended.

Suddenly a familiar tingle shot up from the water, touched his toes and traveled upward into his core. Kit. He closed his eyes and said a silent prayer to the Elysium. The Goddess Varuna might not really care too much, but for her own sense of self-preservation he hoped she would be on this demon's side.

The waters in the middle of the bay parted and Kit arose, the withered body of Queen Elemi in her arms and the amulet hanging around her neck. She had never looked so powerful. So regal.

His body stilled at the force of her presence. Ravanna would have one hell of a fight on his hands.

Kit's legs appeared and she walked toward the shore.

The basilisks hissed, quivering with excitement as she approached but Kit ignored them.

"Stay. Let her pass." Ravanna stood and ushered the beasts behind him, watching as Kit walked in front of him and set her mother on the shore.

She pushed Elemi's hair out of her face. "Breathe," she said. "Breathe the air as you always wanted to, Mother."

The Queen took a deep breath and it rattled in her lungs. She choked and Kit tipped her on her side, letting the water exit her lungs.

Ravanna came to stand before them. "I rather liked having her down there. Much easier on the both of us, don't you think?"

"You were the one who gave her the ability to breathe," said Mane.

"Yes, and I also made sure she stayed alive even though she was too stupid to come up for air. You should be thanking me. I can think of a few ways." Ravanna's tongue snaked out, running across his front teeth, a low growl emanating from the depths of his throat.

Kit patted her mother's back, massaging her and encouraging her to breathe, ignoring Ravanna entirely.

"Mane, please tell your pet she should probably do as I ask her to or she may suffer the consequences."

Kit looked up and saw him for the first time. Her mouth fell open, fingers touching her parted lips. She wanted to scream out, he could feel her pain ripple through his body as their connections strengthened with her desire to help him.

"I would never ask Kit to do anything against her own will, and I know she doesn't want to serve you."

Ravanna shook his head. "You know how thinking turned out before, don't you? If you don't remember, let me remind you." He snapped his fingers and the image of Catherine appeared again, startled as if out of a deep sleep and unable to move. Ankles in chains.

"The woman in the photo. That's her." Kit slowly stood up. Her mother remained lying on her side, breathing in and out in labored gasps.

"I never wanted you to suffer the same fate." He tried using his voice to regain Kit's attention. His plan would not work if her emotions got the best of her. She winked, answering the call strengthened by their blood bond. Without a word she drew out her sword, not taking her eyes from him.

"Oh, you certainly have a live one. This will be fun." Ravanna's voice deepened as he took a step toward Kit. "I could fuck her over her mother's dying body. What a fitting start to our union. Gives me the chills."

A sword would do nothing to Ravanna. He knew that. More importantly, Kit knew. She closed her palm over the blade and pulled up. Blood dripped from her hand into the water at her feet.

He dipped his toe down and felt the magic of their connection call out to him through her blood. He could only hope she understood.

With all his being he reached out through their connection and spoke in his mind over and over. "Don't worry. Don't worry. Don't worry, sweet Kit. This end is only the beginning. You will be okay."

⋙⋘

Kit felt Ravanna inching closer. She froze, sword in hand. Each drop of blood coerced her demon to the surface. Evil drank in the cinnabar cocktail and pushed her in a direction she didn't want to go but knew she must. A hellish homing beacon sending her straight into Ravanna's arms.

Her eyes locked onto Mane and she watched as he stretched his foot out, touching the water and letting out a sigh. Her blood had reached him. She felt a calm suddenly settle over her. The calm she only felt with Mane.

He stared at her and the muscles in his shoulders tensed. She felt the shudder of her mother's body expelling the last of the waters of Mavrovo as the tree Mane was tied to fell forward.

Ravanna broke out in malevolent laughter. "Die, asshole. I've got another soulless sack waiting for you."

Her lover thrashed around in the water. She took a step toward Mane and Elemi grabbed her ankle. Opposing emotions warred within her. Mane counted on her to end this. Her beast threatened to end everything in sight, snarling from deep within her caged soul. The water went still. She sensed no pain through their bond, no fear, only peace. She couldn't save him. She looked down at her mother. Queen Elemi, the color returning to her cheeks, lay at her feet. "Please," she whispered.

Ravanna continued to laugh, certainly proud of himself, confident nothing could defeat him. The only person fated to change that was Valora, but it didn't mean Kit couldn't wreck his plans. Even at the price of her sanity, saving the Realms made the sacrifice worthwhile.

Elemi's blackened pupils transformed into her human disguise as she used her remaining strength to reflect the mother she never could be. For the last time. "This is your destiny, my child."

Vision narrowed to a small tunnel where only her target was in focus. Dry, uncontrolled sobs erupted from her core.

"Now!" yelled her mother.

She drew the sword from her waist and plunged it into her mother's heart.

"No!" Ravanna reached out and then staggered backward, an invisible force pulling him down to his knees.

Elemi beckoned her forward. A keening pain flowed faster than the blood from her hands, faster than the air rushing from her mother's lungs. Elemi placed a hand around the back of her neck and drew her closer, whispering into her ear.

"You have finally fulfilled the real selkie prophecy. Congratulations, my daughter. I always knew you would bring the selkie into their rightful place."

With the final confusing words, her mother took her last breaths in her daughter's arms.

༄⚬ᢙ

Mane could sense the activity all around him, but he needed to concentrate. He searched out what he had seen through the depths below his feet. Diving down, he thrashed around until he found the sharp edge as it sliced into the side of his cheek.

He rose up and positioned his body so the horns on his helm cut into the ropes instead of his flesh. Sawing back and forth, the binds snapped one by one.

His physical body lost the fight to breathe in at the same moment he won the fight with his binds and burst out of the water.

The waters at the heart of the bay began to churn, ever expanding circles surrounding the ankles of Ravanna who stood in the center of the bay trying to escape. He reached out to his basilisks who took a step forward and were pulled into the swirling waters. At the eye of the forming vortex was Ravanna who was anything but calm.

Kit stayed at the edge, clutching her mother's lifeless body to her chest, the sword lodged in her mother's heart. It might as well have been within Kit's chest. He felt her pain and the sorrow taking over.

"Kit, you need to get out of the water," he yelled. He wanted to get her to safety, but the pull of Acheron echoed through the waves and sank a hook into his demon. The current ripped at his feet and he grabbed his helm before it could be swept away. He used their tree to drag himself up onto the shore, hoping the limp limbs would hang on just a little longer.

One strong thrust and he sank his fingers into the sandy shore of Mavrovo.

Looking back he saw Kit in the shallows, refusing to let go of her mother. The water swirled around faster and faster. Two more turns and she would be swept along with it.

He couldn't help her. She needed to help herself.

Once on the shore, he knelt down before her. She was only ten feet from him. So close and yet too far for him to reach. At least not with his body.

"Kit, listen to me."

She raised her head from her mother's body, the look on her face as shattered and broken as her heart. Her body swayed back and forth as the waters threatened to pull her down.

"I need you to fight, Kit. Please."

"But why? This was my purpose. I've done it. She even said so."

"We're not done, Kit. Can't you feel it? We're not done." He touched his cheek, taking a few drops of the blood from his cut, and touched the edge of the water.

Kit froze, her eyes locked with his, and slowly released her hold on her mother. The waters took the body, sucking it down into the vortex.

She clutched her chest and reached out her hand. "Please, please, please," she muttered under her breath.

He cradled the helm in his hands. If he had to sacrifice

himself to save Kit, he would. She accepted her fate and so would he. Placing the helm on his head he took a step into the waters, half expecting the force to pull him forward.

"Glad to see you will both be joining me in Acheron," yelled Ravanna. Only his head remained above the water line. Killing Elemi broke the connection. Somehow Kit knew what needed to be done and now the power was being consumed by some unknown force.

His foot turned to lead as it hit the water. He focused his mind on his target. Kit. He needed to get to her. Only five more steps. Even if this was his last moment here in the Realms he would be sustained into the next millennia knowing he had the love of this woman.

With that thought Kit suddenly fell into his arms. He stood strong, the waters pulling at his legs but unable to bring him down.

"It's not possible. Not possible," yelled Ravanna. The waters battered against him and he held Kit to his chest, waiting for the current to take them both as he took his last comfort in her and gave her his embrace and love in return. She would know in her last moments that no matter what she had done she was good, she deserved love, and she had it with him.

A bolt of lightning cracked across the sky and touched down in the waters at his feet sending a jolt across their bodies and blasting him backward. He fell with a great force against the ground, rolling with Kit's body curled up against him.

The basilisks shrieked as they were all pulled downward and the center of the vortex opened wide. Ravanna slipped downward and a blast of lightning struck again, closing the portal once more. The waters stilled. Everything went silent. The clouds above their heads parted and gentle rays of sun cast down onto the beach warming his skin.

A shudder passed through Kit. She was moving and alive. The amulet at her throat glowed deep blue. It belonged to her now. Last of the selkie.

❧

"We seem to end up on this shore a lot." Kit looked up into Mane's eyes and soaked in every ounce of joy and life pulsing through their newly formed blood bond.

"Yes, my Queen, but today is different."

The words did nothing to comfort her. She struggled from his arms and stood up, looking out over the waters. The cinnabar was disappearing, but the waters of Mavrovo were still red. They would be for a while. Too much blood had been spilled. If only she had listened to her mother earlier and led her people out of the waters, she would not be the last of the selkie. She would not be Queen.

"I never wanted any of it." Some girls dreamed of living in a fairytale world with magic, castles, dragons, and a knight in shining armor. She never once dreamt of those things, only a normal life. Walking to school without running out of breath. Going to a friend's birthday party and not having to worry she would have an episode. Kissing a boy who wanted to kiss her back without worrying he might catch her illness. She didn't ask for this life.

Mane gathered her up into his arms again and she didn't have the strength to struggle. Not physically or emotionally. "Neither did I."

She clutched the one man who knew her. All of her. The bad and the good, listened to him echo her words and wishes for something more than what they had now.

Pushing thoughts of her mother and Ravanna as far back into the recesses of her mind as she could she held him tighter. She could have lost Mane today. Forever. That could just as easily happen tomorrow or the next day. The end of everything seemed to be so close and she only wanted Mane closer.

"How will we ever have a normal life?" She pressed her lips to his chest and kissed up the center, relishing the feel of his heart beating strong and alive.

He let out a groan and pressed against her, his growing need unmistakable. "I think before we try and figure that out we should enjoy this moment together. Who knows when life will slow to this pace again." His hands worked their way from her shoulders down the length of her body. Cupping her bare bottom he pulled her up into his arms, her back pressed against something hard behind her.

"You don't care? I said I wanted to be normal." Despite craving all the answers she couldn't help but feel the switch inside her. The one that could go from off to on in a second with one flick of Mane's fingers. And he had already electrified the circuit.

He pulled back, keeping his weight against her as he took her face in his hands. "Sweetheart, just because neither of us wants to deal with magic, demons, or eternal life doesn't mean we have to become vanilla."

He reached behind her and quickly brought a rope underneath her breasts, tugging upward and letting the rough cord bite into her skin as she had bit into him.

Pain and pleasure, mixed up in one delicious package. If she could have her cake and eat it too, nothing would stop her from indulging.

He wound a second rope around the top of her breasts and let her feet sink to the ground. "Where did you happen to find all this handy binding material?"

Mane brought her arms up and affixed her wrists above

her head with a quick handcuff knot.

"Our tree." Mane reached up and plucked a fruit from above her head. Its purplish skin looked as healthy and sweet as the first day she spied them from the water's edge, the day she met Mane and fell in love with him forever.

He brought the fruit to her lips and gently prodded them open. Her tongue danced across the soft skin. "Is it safe?"

Mane raised one eyebrow and displayed a wide grin. "When is safe ever fun?"

She looked at him over the top of the fruit and opened her mouth wide, sinking her teeth deep into the sweet flesh, its juices running down the sides of her mouth. She swallowed, relishing the flavor, relishing the moment.

Mane lapped up the juices on the sides of her mouth before kneeling down and lapping up every bit of pleasure and sound he could evoke from her. One lifetime of this might be all she could take. And even in those unrestrained moments she knew it would be enough. He would be enough.

Hours later they lay entwined on the beach watching the sun setting at the time it should, without any undue influence. Deep within Mane's embrace she felt safe, but she knew the guilt associated with all the death she witnessed and had been a part of would come flooding back soon enough. Ravanna was no longer an immediate threat to the Realms, but he remained a threat. He would find a way back.

As if in answer to her thoughts a low humming emanated from Mane's vest.

"What is that?"

Mane rummaged through his pocket and withdrew a small broken section of mirror. She recognized a familiar face reflected back, one who probably wouldn't want to see her.

"Mind if I take this?" asked Mane.

She withdrew her legs from his and sat up. She watched as he took a few steps and spoke to the man in the mirror. The feelings of guilt were coming back and coming back strong.

Mane shoved the mirror back into his pocket. "There may be a problem Earthside. We need to get back to Dell'Aria and warn Valora and the others."

The sun dipped lower in the sky. The final curtain call. She looked up at their tree. It had fallen into the waters and somehow after all was said and done it was back in its rightful place acting as part of the magical border between Mavrovo and the Riparian. It knew its place and even when knocked down it got back up again. Because it had no choice. Because it was meant to be. Because she and Mane were meant to be.

She wound her arms around him and he did the same, pulling her in close. Darkness descended but even without a light she knew their direction. "We will go back. But they need time to prepare." He pressed into her with ease. "And so do we."

Thank you for reading *Mane Chance*.

If you enjoyed *Mane Chance*, please consider helping others to enjoy this book as well.

- **Recommend it.** Please help other readers find this book by recommending it to friends, readers groups, and discussion boards.
- **Review it.** Please tell other readers why you liked this book by reviewing it at one of the following websites: Amazon, Barnes and Noble, or Goodreads.

Mane Chance is a novella set within the Realms, a world created for the Soulstealer Trilogy. If you like Mane and Kit's story and would like to see what happens next, you can read the continuation of their adventures in *Fae Warrior (The Soulstealer Trilogy, Book #3)*. If you missed the first other three book in the series, don't forget to check out *Fae Hunter (The Soulstealer Trilogy, Book #1)*, *Mane Attraction (A Soulstealer Novella, Book #1.5)*, and *Fae Guardian (The Soulstealer Trilogy, Book #2)*.

FAE HUNTER (*The Soulstealer Trilogy, Book #1*)

Valora Delos is a Hunter, charged with tracking the treacherous Soulstealers and bringing them to justice. Unlike the other fae of her kind, Valora was born with stunted wings that render her flightless, driving her to prove herself in the eyes of King Aric, with whom she has been infatuated since she first set eyes on him as a young prince.

She descends to Earth and finds herself trapped in suburban Seattle after the portal to her world closes. With the help of a sexy half-fae named Dooley, Valora must find her way back to save Dell'Aria. Dooley uses his own brand of magic to help Valora discover memories buried deep within her, which produce more questions than answers-questions about her growing attraction to Dooley and her devotion to her King. Uncovering who the Soulstealers are and who is behind the destruction of Dell'Aria brings Valora a truth she may not be able to handle.

MANE ATTRACTION *(A Soulstealer Novella, Book #1.5)*

Being a demon trapped in an elves body seemed a prison at first, but Mane has gotten used to his new home in the Riparian forest amongst the elves. When the waters of Lake Mavrovo start to run red it seems a sure sign that the demon king that cast him out may rise again. In order to investigate he will need to navigate the dominion of the selkie, and they aren't known for playing nice.

Going from an apartment in the suburbs of Seattle to living in a castle at the bottom of a lake in the Realms was one change that Kit had to get used to, being half-selkie was another. Now she has to get used to the changes she undergoes after the the selkie sleep. One that involves bloodlust and lust of a whole different kind. A problem she is hoping Mane will help her with.

FAE GUARDIAN *(The Soulstealer Trilogy, Book #2)*

Dealing with wedding day woes, naked elven rituals, a best friend with a biting problem, dragon battles, and a war brewing between the selkie and the fae are only the beginning for Valora, the Fae Guardian.

Valora needs to get Aric out of her mind if she's going to live happily ever after with Dooley. But nothing is ever easy with magic. Tying herself and Dooley to Aric becomes a matter of life and death, not just for them but for all of the Realms and even those beyond the portals to Earth.

But can Valora handle the affections of two half-fae brothers? She has to if she wants to save the Realms -- a world filled with cloud cities, volcanic mountains mined by dwarves, deserts inhabited by dragons, and lakes teaming with ferocious selkie. And getting the two of them to get along may be her biggest battle yet.

FAE WARRIOR (The Soulstealer Trilogy, Book #3)

Valora Delos – a fae of Dell'Aria – has spent her life battling the unknown foe responsible for her mother's death. Now she is racing against the clock to keep Ravanna, the Demon King of Acheron, from invading the Realms. Drowning in the affections from two half-fae brothers in a tricky magical triad turned love triangle doesn't help matters. Cryptic prophecies and cagey spells take Valora through hell and back. As if that weren't enough – someone else's agenda could prevent Valora from being the one to "save us all."

CHECK OUT A SNEAK PEEK OF
THE LAST BOOK IN THE SOULSTEALER
SERIES:

FAE WARRIOR

CHAPTER ONE

"Taking a break already, Valora?" Orris poked his head through the turret of the nearest wall tower, his usual greasy brown locks washed and pulled back into a low ponytail. After the sting of his brother's death dissipated, the stench of poor hygiene worked like smelling salts to snap him back into action. He brought a butterbread to his mouth and took a large bite, letting the slight afternoon breeze blow the crumbs down upon the passersby below.

For the first time, I sat atop the wall walk with no motivation other than to watch over the people of Dell'Aria. To truly be their Guardian whether I was allowed to or not. As a child I played along the tops of the stone battlements to escape the prying eyes of those who viewed me as different and someone who should never have been allowed to live. When I got older, balancing along the narrow ledge proved my agility to the naysayers. Even without the wings of a full fae, I could have served in the King's Guard. Now that I am considered a Princess, I can't technically be a Guardian. I'm not sure what to call myself anymore. Especially with my fate spelled out in the well-worn page tucked deep in my pocket.

"No, Orris, I've been practicing all morning while you've been eating butterbreads no doubt." I used my copper short sword for leverage to push myself to standing. Having found out the hard way that drawing a sword takes longer than getting hit, I always have my blade at the ready.

Each time a fae fell before me in battle, I felt the sharp pain of their death branded into my skull. I wouldn't forget, I couldn't forget. Any of them. Many had died, some because of me, and the throbbing ache refused to subside — a second pulse beating along with those who survived. Now more than ever, I felt prepared to ready a city and myself for battle.

"This is my first one. I've got a break from my watch if you want to practice your swing." He shoved the remainder of the cake into his mouth and swallowed hard. Orris, once my bitter enemy, now my sworn ally and protector. If his motivations included my newly minted title of Princess, I wouldn't accept his loyalties, but Orris' devotion ran deeper. I tried to save his brother and he never reminded me I failed.

"If you lose any more feathers I think my father will take my sword. Another time."

Orris shrugged and disappeared into the castle.

Everyone readies for battle in a different way. Dooley had magic, Aric had wings, and I had a sword. Whatever was happening, the three of us were meant to fight together. We were linked by our amulets and drew power from one another. However, Dooley now spent all his time with Pryn, learning spells and studying any text that might help us defeat Ravanna, the Demon King of Acheron. And then there was Aric.

"Alright ladies, we call this one the Ustrasana." In the courtyard below, Aric led some of the fae women through a series of exercises he called yoga. "Naked yoga." Leave it to

Aric to find another excuse to show off his body. And leave it to my wandering eyes to want to linger.

"Really push forward so you can get a deep back bend." Aric modeled the pose, pushing his bare pelvis forward. The memory of tracing each line of muscle cutting across his stomach made my fingers tingle. Once a lover, now a friend, both he and Dooley were untouchable to me now. I set aside my regrets and forced my mind on other more pressing matters.

Aric had become the center of attention again after the revelation that he had the blessing of the Goddess Varuna. Despite his initial shunning of fame, he soon realized, better they worship at your feet than take your head. And he ingratiated himself deeper into their hearts by providing a welcome diversion from the burbling waters of Lake Mavrovo. The blood red depths were a constant reminder of the impending apocalypse that threatened our floating fortress. I appreciated his presence as a much needed distraction to those who couldn't fight. And for some of us who can. I pushed that thought to the back of my mind. My father, the King, might not like Aric's latest endeavor, but our priests, including Pryn, welcomed his silly diversion. Because of him, they didn't need to waste time counseling the panicked masses.

Aric stood, directing his attention to a passing cart loaded down with weapons as the voluptuous hips of one of the older fae pressed towards him. Elderly women, none shy about their bodies, occupied the entire front row. The young girls, I'm sure he hoped would attend, were nowhere to be seen. I covered my mouth, biting my lips to hide my smile. The movement caught the attention of his roving eye.

"Valora!" He gestured to his new found disciples. "You're all dismissed. Go home and prostrate yourself in

reverence to the Goddess Varuna. We'll resume tomorrow."
The front row stood, covering my view of Aric's naked
lower half. Despite my better judgment, I searched through
the spaces between the women to get a better look when he
slipped his legs into supple white leather pants. My mouth
suddenly ran as dry as the Ordos Desert and hotter than the
dragons residing there. His eyes locked with mine as he tied
to the white silken straps of his vest across his sculpted
torso.

He spread the soft blue feathers of his wings and shot
gracefully into the air. His effortless movement made my
heart skip a beat. I caught my breath before he landed beside
me.

"Like what you saw?" One eyebrow cocked as he leaned
against the parapet. He swept a hand through his hair, and
flipped the ice blond locks over his shoulder.

"Are you kidding? You have every old marm in
Dell'Aria naked and at your beckon call. I liked what I saw
because it's hilarious." I ducked around him to head into the
keep. My bed called to me and my forced celibacy meant
avoiding this conversation. The sun signaled midday, not a
time for turning in, but sleep had eluded me the night before
— a common occurrence these days. He reached out,
grabbing me by the wrist and pulled me a few steps toward
him. Talented fingers trailed down my temple, gently tucking
a loose auburn curl behind my ear. "Then why are you
sweating?"

I swatted at his hand. "Because I've been practicing all
morning. Some of us are actually trying to prepare for what's
to come." Aric followed close behind, his breath tickling the
back of my neck, the silk of his vest cool on my heated
wings. He knew all too well how to weaken my resolve. As
long as I avoided eye contact I might make it to my bedroom

without having to deflect his advances.

"Don't get angry with me, Valora. It's not my fault Kit and Mane have been gone so long. That is what's really bothering you, right?"

The disappearance of my friends was only one of my worries. Hot tears welled up in the corner of my eyes and I forced them to stop. Despite the protective bubble I erected around my thoughts, Aric could read me like a book. Showing weakness in front of him would be all the consent he needed to push things even further. And sleeping with him would be suicide because of the tension between the three of us.

The relationship between Dooley, Aric, and I remained unspoken. Reopening old wounds slows down the healing process. *Our success against Ravanna necessitated we work together.* Dooley's voice echoed inside my head, his painful mantra meant to keep me emotionally and physically at a distance. To push me away.

Following the path towards my room, I skirted the practice arena. The rosy scent of a dozen pairs of wings perfumed with naughty thimbleberry blooms blocked my escape route. Before me a hall packed full of hormonal adolescents and lonesome spinsters clamored to see over one another into the arena.

"Your students must have gotten lost." I pressed through the crowd and the chattering and giggling abruptly stopped. Keen silence, and a particularly full pair of lilac wings, halted my forward progression. Even before I rose on my tiptoes, I knew the local celebrity causing the blockade.

Dooley stood several feet from me in the middle of the dusty practice arena, his once blue jeans now covered in black markings from his practice of the symbol magic. The tops of his hip bones were exposed just enough to remind me of the anatomy below his loose belt line. His tan skin glowed, sparkling in the midday light. Swirls of black sand drifted up lazily from a pile at his feet. His magnetic fingers moved with the purpose of a practiced performer, drawing the audience and the particles of ash dust into the palm of his hand.

The sand formed symbols in the air, something I'd never seen him do. Excitement rippled through the crowd at the sight. A fae girl with pink wings took in a sharp breath, and grabbed her friend's arm in awe.

I felt much the same as I watched his brown eyes blacken, pupils wide and liquid like the last time he kissed me. The memory made my legs weak and my body reissued the threat of giving out. The floor tilted. Aric rushed to my side, using the length of his body to brace me before I toppled into the crowd. I wished he were Dooley. The amulet at my neck flared to life — an unmistakable siren signaling my weakened state. I closed my hand around the shining red stone and tried to shove the blazing beacon down the front of my bodice to escape the notice of all those around me. I didn't escape his notice though.

The sand splashed down to the floor and a plume of dust parted the sea of women who stood aside to let Dooley through. Relief flooded my limbs. If I had known I needed to resort to fainting to get that man's attention, I would have done it earlier.

Aric pulled me to his chest and whispered into my ear. "You're exhausted. Let me take you to your room."

Dooley's concerned stare turned to stone, but his stride lengthened in rigid determination.

I shut my eyes to stop the room from spinning. Aric gathered me up into his arms like a child, my exhaustion winning the war over common sense. I didn't want Dooley to get the wrong idea but I was tired of trying to figure everything out and wired with unspent adrenaline. I might die before the war even started. There were days I would go without any sleep and times that the fae my father charged with keeping the "princess" tended to could barely pull me out of bed.

"I could use a little nap."

The scent of labdanum resin with its heady notes of wood, earth and smoke caught my nose and heightened my senses, making me aware of Dooley's presence even before he spoke. "I'll take her."

"I can make sure she gets to bed safely," Aric's chest puffed out like some overinflated Sage Grouse. The show was over for the fae women who I could feel shooting jealous daggers at me for my dilemma.

"I'll take her." Dooley's tone was flat and even, no sign that he cared one way or the other for me, only that he fulfilled his duty. After what happened between the three of us, I understood the reasons behind his anger. Even now, the sight of me in Aric's arms evoked only an uncomfortable silence. How had we drifted this far apart from where we used to be?

Aric let out a long, low sigh and carefully deposited me into another set of arms. "I'll humor you this time. Rest up, Valora."

A second scent clung to Dooley's skin, layered beneath the labdanum. The potent smell of vetiver both he and Pryn explained was normal. I never forgot my late uncle's warning. To Artemus, vetiver bespoke of something to come. Something bad. Exhaustion overcame worry. To have just one night of sleep. One night where dreams did not drift towards the two men before me. Focusing on the mission would be much easier if I knew where we stood. But I wasn't going to let my selfish needs take precedence over the safety of the Realms.

Dooley laid me onto my bed and covered my shoulders with a light blanket. Seconds later the click of the latch signaled his departure. No kiss on my forehead, no whisper of soothing words.

Nothing.

Makeshift darkness descended along with the heavy quilt over my head. The fetal position is usually comforting except when you have a rolled sheaf of paper poking into your gut. I dug into my pocket and pulled out the parchment from the book I found in Mane's apartment. The book, supposedly written by Pryn, was about the wars between Varuna and Ravanna. I unfolded the page again and read for the hundredth time the prophecy which told me no matter how much I wanted to hide under these covers and cry, I wouldn't be able to hide for long. Pryn's premonition echoed in my ears as I drifted to sleep. *You will save us all.*

���

A deep voice curled in and out of me, sending titillating vibrations where they shouldn't be. "Valora. Sweet, sweet Valora. I warned you I would come. I'm getting closer and there is nothing you can do to stop me. Your weak attempts to keep me trapped in Acheron will fail. There is no greater power than mine and you are foolish to think you can defeat me. No magic user alive can match me. Not Pryn and definitely not my son."

Eyes open, I found myself running along a familiar path through the woods. Tree limbs whipped at my face and I pushed past them towards my destination. I didn't stop until I reached the roughhewn cabin tucked amongst the deep green rain forest. Dooley stood tall on the wide porch, a shotgun slung over his shoulder. Relief shot through me. I would be safe here. Safe with him. My hand on the stair rail, I raised my foot to the bottom step when a distinctive click halted me in mid-motion. Dooley aimed a shotgun at the center of my forehead, his eyes glowing with the demon light of Acheron. Before I could react, a black hand shot up from the mud at my feet and pulled me down — sinking through layers of suffocating earth into pure heat.

I bolted upright and clenched my fists in sweat soaked sheets. The feathers of my wings were askew and badly in need of a shower. The light of the early morning coming through the open window and last night's dinner setting cold on the table told me I had slept through the day and night. Ravanna showing up in my dreams shouldn't have been a surprise. I tried to prepare myself. But you can't really prepare for a disaster. You can only pretend to be ready and then when the real time comes, only inner strength and resolve would carry you through. An empty pit in my stomach grew in place of resolve. Of course no matter how many scenarios you have run through your head, the reality is always ten times worse.

A short series of raps sounded at the door before someone opened it an inch. "Are you decent? Better if you're not, but I thought I would show the expected courtesy to a fae princess."

"Mane!" I shoved the crumpled scroll under my pillow and jumped out of bed. Mane pushed the door the rest of the way open.

From the moment I met the demon he wore an air of superiority. He stood tall through the most difficult times, but now a slight slump to his shoulders marred his proud stance. His skin smelled of lilac, Kit's perfume, and his plain linen tunic stretched tight across his muscular chest. My natural inclination was to ask him how he planned to sit in his painted on pants without splitting himself in two. However, instinct told me this was no time for levity. I glanced around, searching for his other half. He was alone.

"Where is Kit?"

Mane rubbed the back of his neck and his casual air disappeared. He looked like he'd lived a thousand lifetimes since I saw him last. The lines under his eyes were the same ones reflected in my own mirror. "She'll be okay. I wouldn't have come here otherwise."

"No, of course not." I'd go to her myself the second I had a chance. I pressed my hands to my stomach, forcing the upset to settle. Mane's unquestionable devotion to Kit brought an unwelcome spark of jealousy. "What did you two find on your journey into Underworld?"

"A nightmare." Mane dropped down onto one of the two low stools in the sitting area to the left of my four poster bed. A small stone table was laden with yet another uneaten meal. Dining alone left me without an appetite.

I often went into town to the local alehouse to share a meal amongst people, even though none of them were my friends. I didn't talk to them, but used the time to remind me of my reasons for going into battle. And to remind them they were not alone. These people depended on my strength. Even though sometimes I felt weak.

"Mind if I take that food off your hands?" Mane gestured to the plate of roast beast, baked knotwood corns, and mashed blue slipper seed.

"No, go ahead. I tried to get my father to have the staff quit bringing the food, but he said serving me was their duty and to deny anyone the thing that kept them busy at a time of impending war would be unwise."

Mane grabbed the meat. He sunk his teeth into the flesh

and his eyes flared red.

"Are you under control?"

My finger fretted with the worn spot at the pommel of my sword. My new nervous habit. A demon in elf's clothing, Mane often reminded me he wasn't evil, but I never could completely trust him. I suppose that was why Dooley, technically part demon also, found it hard to be around me. If my dreams were any indication, my subconscious mind believed Ravanna still resided somewhere within him. If I couldn't trust him, how could he trust me?

"Control has never been a problem for me. Being in Underworld was not good for either Kit or I. But now that we've returned, we can go back to being our normal, controlled selves." Mane gave me a slightly flirtatious grin. Now *that* was the demon I knew. "Kit needed some extra assistance from Pryn and Dooley, but she'll be fine." His words seemed to be more to convince him then me. He let the stripped bone clatter onto the plate. "Ravanna has already poisoned the land. There are no creatures left, save the dwarves that are not under his control. The elves have retreated somewhere."

"Where do you think they would go?" The elves weren't our greatest allies, but in this battle we were looking for anything to give us an advantage.

"There's no way to tell. I told my elven brother, Torkel, to come here, but no one has heard from them. Their tracks are lost in all the destruction. They may have even been desperate enough to go to the Ordos Desert."

"Dragonlands." My legs wobbled and I sunk down into the seat next to Mane. "Then we have already lost." Without the dwarves or the elves, I didn't know how we would overtake Ravanna in Underworld.

Mane surveyed the stack of dishes untouched by myself

and the staff. Even the servants were tired of throwing away full plates of food. "You haven't been eating. You need to keep up your strength." He slid the plate towards me and handed me a spoon.

I pushed the vegetables around like I did as a child in the hope that the dispersal of food proved I ate at least a few bites.

Mane stole the spoon from my hand and brought the food to my lips. "No, we haven't lost. If I thought that, I would have jumped the next portal and taken Kit with me. Though that would only buy us a little time."

"I don't believe you would leave us all to Ravanna." I opened my mouth and let the demon feed me the flaccid corns. After a few spoonfuls, the churning in my stomach began to die down.

He paused, taking my hands in his. "You have good intuition."

I gave him a gentle squeeze, glad to know that both he and my friend were safe, for now. "What did you mean that if you left you would only be buying a little time?"

Mane pulled a small portion of mirror out of the pocket of his tight jeans and slid it across the table. "Do you recall when we last left Bowen?"

"Of course." I ran my finger lightly along the rough edge of the broken glass. Bowen, my Uncle Artemus' stepson, knew more than most humans did about our world. We gave him a portion of the talking mirror to get through to us if he ever wanted to. Considering the circumstances, I wasn't sure he would ever want anything to do with our world again. It probably would have been a wise choice for him and for Dooley. I should never have changed the course of his life by letting him come to Dell'Aria.

"He contacted me. There are signs. The same thing is

beginning on Earth. Ravanna left here without much of a fight because he's busy there."

I swallowed, trying to clear the hard lump of food stuck in my throat. "Have you told Dooley and Aric?"

Mane shook his head. "This is not something they can know right now. You and I need to go there first."

"But why?" I couldn't imagine going to Earth without Dooley or Aric.

Mane stood up fast, knocking his chair to the ground. "Because it involves their mother."

"I know you have some personal experience with possessing the body of another, but their mother had her memory wiped. She doesn't know anything about the Goddess Varuna or Ravanna having possessed her. She doesn't even remember Dooley or Aric. It was the only way to keep her safe." Underneath Kit's perfume the scent of fear clung to Mane.

He glanced down at the talking mirror used to communicate between long distances. And the message on the other end of this one came from a world as far from the Realms as you could get.

"She's starting to remember."

ABOUT THE AUTHOR

Photo by Phil Holden

Nicolette is a mother, wife, paralegal, writer, knitter, traveler, violinist and anything else she can get her hands on. She turned to writing stories at an early age, when filling out Mad Libs just wasn't enough.

She enjoys watching dark comedies, warped fairytales, and cheesy 80s comedies. Her interest in music spans from George Winston to Thrill Kill Cult to Bel Canto and U2. She loves to travel, and plans to do more as her son grows older. In her younger days she loved to go out dancing, and you may still, on occasion find her shaking her booty during 80s or goth rock nights at the few clubs they still exist at. She is constantly picking up new hobbies and interests. She knits socks, grows mini cucumbers in her garden, and played the violin for 5 years. She has a pug dog with a nervous temperament and speaks a little Spanish. She's eclectic.

Please come visit Nicolette Reed at: www.nicolettereed.com